The Rules of Falling

Grace Harrison

Contents

Chapter 1

There's a fine line between knowing what you need and what you want. I learned that sometime ago, long before anyone else had separated these two essential facts of life.

I always balanced my life accordingly, pushing aside what I didn't need at the moment and putting my mind to building a sturdy foundation for my life. My mother's friends called me a poster child—the kind of kid they dreamed of raising.

That's just the thing, you can only teach what you know, and my mother was a professional at sorting out her priorities.

Call it what you will, murmur under your breath about how the apple doesn't fall far from the tree, because you're exactly right. My mother buried herself in work, wasted no time with mindless tasks, spent most of her time elbow deep in some city project or volunteer assignment—ended up being the most hardworking, involved mayor Ashwood Creek has ever seen.

No dilly-dally, straight up, blunt, and unnaturally good—that's how she operated. I think the only crazy thing she ever did in her life was get knocked up. And, well, that began the story of me: Jovie Underwood—unexpected, somewhat embarrassing result of a one night stand with my mother's assistant.

Now, of course, she had years to come to terms with the fact that a dedicated, otherwise hardworking woman like herself, made a mistake one night in a moment of weakness. My father—or Henry as I refer to him as—on the other hand, couldn't be prouder of the fact he hooked up with my mother and ended up with me.

You see, his mad crush on her still lives on to this day, but she doesn't ever acknowledge their previous engagement unless it boils down to me.

I liked to think off them as a tragic love story—my mother: a headstrong woman entirely devoted to her work fell for the charm of her secretary, a carefree man who was madly in love with her, and gave in to what she thought would be a harmless night of fun only to discover herself pregnant and forever bound to him by the ties of their daughter despite her efforts to forget their rendezvous.

And, while the tragic love story idea is attractive, it's called tragic for a reason. The thing I learned from my parents was to distinguish between need and want. What's necessary, what's luxury, and how that choice would ultimately affect me.

Because I am so much like my mother, I always chose need and spent most of my life throwing myself into education and friendships I only deemed beneficial. I didn't have time for drama, I didn't have time for distractions. I was a spinning wheel, and nothing could slow me down or sway me off my course.

When I met Bash, however, my wheel began to teeter. I suddenly understood what weakness felt like. I started losing control, became reckless in my own way. It seemed the only thing I could get a good grasp on was the idea of graduation looming over my shoulder.

That was our expiration date. Like a one night stand, Bash and I needed to know our limitations. We knew it would end—and it did.

Tragic.

I didn't want him to go. I didn't want him to understand how I operated. I didn't want to be so much like my mother. But, I needed to be.

Drama, distractions, no way. I couldn't. So, we said good-bye.

I don't regret it, though. Being with him let me experience what a relief letting go was, how closing my eyes and blindly choosing want was exhilarating, nearly trance inducing.

I didn't need him. I never needed him. He was always pure want, pure heart-pounding, gut-wrenching desire. Not like that passionate stuff they make up in the movies, a real friendship, true excitement, magnetic. He made me happy. He taught me things. Some were trivial like big words, but mostly sensations: spontaneity, craving.

I was programmed to be a machine, taught to do what was expected, what looked right. I'm still this way because you can't completely change a person, but now I know what straight up freedom tastes like—how letting my hair down and heart open allowed me to really breathe.

It was worth it.

Maybe I can have all of that again someday, but not now. It's not the time. What I can do is reminisce, marvel at what we were: Bash and I.

There was nothing special about the day I met Bash—there hardly ever is anything important about the weather or events leading up to those sorts of occasions.

No ray of sunshine shone through a ceiling to floor length window to announce how important he would become in my life, no ominous clouds and thunder to announce the kind of pain our separation would cause me. No warning signs, no hints, not even intuition. In fact, I didn't even realize we made a connection until days later, but that's getting too far ahead.

Let me start with that morning. There's a handful of things to note. Mid-summer in Ashwood Creek is one of the most unbearable times of the year. The humidity makes you sticky, no amount of deodorant makes you socially presentable, and most people find themselves falling into a horrible habit of barring themselves up in their air-conditioned homes for comfort's sake.

I seemed to be living on the wrong street of the city to make any of these things true.

Our next door neighbor owned chickens, presented for the entire neighborhood to see in a pen displayed, non-other, than on her front lawn. They were horrible, loud things that made strange foreign noises when you walked outside. Otherwise, they spent most of their time squawking and being insufferable.

Across the street was an old man whom I'd never actually met, but spent nearly all of his time on his front porch under an awning singing show tunes to his heart's content while shucking pea pods. Whenever I got the mail he'd wave and yell a cheery hello.

There were very few people I bothered with, but I maintained a friendship with Quinn Alberstein, a girl from down the block, to help pass the time during summer and enlighten me on normal teen behavior during the school year. She was unavoidable growing up. Her mother babysat me when mine went back to work. Sisters is probably a better word to describe our relationship and explains why we put up with each other.

Anyway, it had come to that point in the summer where being cooped up indoors was a bore, the chickens were intolerable, awkward interaction with the Pea Shucker was off-putting, and being roped into another session of lifeguard stalking with Quinn at the local waterpark was no longer an appealing idea that I decided I needed to find something to do outside my neighborhood.

So, I hopped on the bike Henry gifted me years back to encourage my visits during the weekdays, and braved the humidity in search for a more productive way to spend my summer.

I hadn't planned on ending up in the library, I only went inside because I'd been biking for a fair amount of time, and it was the one place I knew that offered: a) air-conditioning b) a bubbler c) a comfortable chair I could rest in.

So, I locked my bike up and climbed the cracked steps up to the heavy doors of Merriweather Public Library. Note that I wasn't looking to meet anyone special that day. I was a sight for sore eyes with my frizzy near-black hair pulled into a sloppy bun on the top of my head, last-minute decision strappy tank top, faded flip-flops, and perspiration from the bike ride lingering at my hairline. But, I was there for a breather only.

Merriweather Public Library hadn't changed one bit since the last time I was there—which had only been earlier that year for study prep—but is always something I feel like I need to make a point of saying when I haven't been somewhere for an extended period of time.

The women at the front desk waved to me when I walked past, and the sun beat down on me through the skylight windows as I walked up the stairs to the upper level where I knew the water fountain was.

After spending an enormously obnoxious length of time at the bubbler refreshing myself, I found a comfy chair to sit, appreciating the cool leather when my bare skin came in contact with it. For a moment I just sat and stared out at the few people browsing books or sitting at computers. I felt myself gradually begin to cool off and relax, and I decided that while I was there I could humor myself with a walk around. So, just as quickly as I sat down, I got back up and strode toward the nearest aisle of books.

For whatever reason, I got invested fast. Soon, I was standing on tip-toes to read the titles on the top shelf, ducked low to see those hiding on the bottom, and lightly touched the spines of every book I could.

I got this sort of childish giddiness from it, something I forgot happened when scouring the library. It was easy to forget my surroundings and pretend like nothing else exsisted. It was just me and thousands of books I hadn't touched.

I barely noticed him at first. He was so quiet, weaving his way around the aisles, packing books tightly in their place, and somehow managing to stop the cart wheels from squealing as he went. In fact, I didn't notice I was in another person's presence until I found myself nearly bumping into him.

I shuffled back apologetically after almost running him over and mumbled an awkward "sorry", because I could only imagine being in his place. The amount of times people had been inconsiderate to my presence annoyed me, and I hated being on the giving end of that action.

He sent me a brief half-smile and turned back to finding where the book in his hand belonged. It occurred to me, then, how young he was—only a few years older than I—and yet he was stacking books in the library. My eyebrows crinkled together at that, a peculiar site as it was—a young man stacking books when a woman nearing retirement was usually the one on the job—but it wasn't the only strange thing about him. He seemed oddly aloof, his entire posture relaxed even though I had just invaded his personal space.

I would expect him to be more rigid—the way I would normally react, the way I'd always seen others react. But, no awkward tension between us presented itself. I could stand there forever, probably as close as I like, and he wouldn't even blink. He was too busy with the task at hand to care.

Intrigued, and admittedly curious about him, I snuck a glance, eyes lingering long enough to make note of his features. His face tilted away from mine, blonde hair just long enough to be tied back, making high cheek bones jut out and jaw appear sharper than is probably was. The slope of his nose was short, sitting high on his face. A little higher, yet, were wide eyes under thin brows. A skinny lower lip was sucked under his teeth, being chewed on slowly as if in thought as he searched for the place a book entitled Living Proof belonged. Finally, his eyes slid toward me, and I realized I'd been staring.

I cleared my throat and quickly moved my eyes elsewhere.

"Do you need something?" He asked.

My cheeks flushed at his question, embarrassed that I'd made him acknowledge me, and also aware of how frightening I must look. I cared very much how he would perceive me—and in that moment, I knew there was a great chance that I was accidentally making myself look like a fool. I'd already ran into him, and now I was staring.

"No," I answered and wrapped my arms across my chest, hand sweeping across my forehead to smooth down any frizzy baby hairs.

He abruptly turned to the cart at his hip and pulled a book from the stack, extending it to me.

"If you can't find anything," he said, "I found this to be quite mesmeric."

I couldn't stop the short laugh that broke forth from my lips as I took the book from him. "Mesmeric?" I asked of his interesting choice in language.

A smile stretched across his face. "Cool word, right? It means fascinating."

I nodded and turned the book over in my hands. It was worn hardcover, practically falling apart in my hands with yellowing pages and an old book smell reeking from it. The title scrawled across the top was gold, elaborate calligraphy spelling: The Lost City.

"Atlantis?" I shook my head and gave the book a quick page through.

"It's supposedly based off of a real documentary." His eyes grew a little, giving away the fact that he didn't believe a word of it. "But, storyline is absolutely prodigious."

"Mesmeric, prodigious..." I chuckled lightly and raised an eyebrow. "Are you sure you're using those right, or are just trying to sound smart?"

He rested a forearm atop the cart and pursed his lips at me. "Ye of little faith."

There was a fair amount of challenge in his voice. He seemed confident he knew what he was talking about, and I knew I sounded snobbish instead of playful—which was both accidental and on purpose. The word "mesmeric" was endearing until "prodigious" followed. I found a certain kind of annoyance with his use of pretentious vocabulary. He wasn't much older than I, but made sure to sound as though we were decades apart.

I shook my head and looked back down at the book entitled The Lost City, puffing out a short breath.

My lack of response seemed to alert him that our interaction was over and his job was done, so he tapped a finger on the book in my hands and offered a short nod. "Let me know how you like it."

I opened my mouth in an attempt to object because I didn't really want the book he offered, but he placed both hands on the book cart and rolled past me, turning down a different aisle before allowing me to reply.

With a defeated sigh, I carried the book back with me to the chair I started in. Since I was stuck with the book, I thought I'd give it a chance—see for myself if it was truly "mesmeric."

Regrettably, I enjoyed the beginning of that book and came back the following day to check it out, thankful that I didn't run into the young man who suggested it.

So, my first impression of Bash before I even knew him was this: He was a try-hard with good taste in books—and that was that.

Chapter 2

It was a few days later that I went to return The Lost City. I hopped on my bike shortly after my mother left for work and disappeared from the neighborhood for the second time that summer. I even made sure to be a bit more presentable this time, and also remembered my library card.

When I entered the cool building, I quietly slipped the book into the return slot and moved on, eyes flicking in all directions to make sure that the strange librarian from the other day hadn't seen. It's silly, but I felt a little at war with him, and taking that book meant he was winning.

I was still holding his pompousness against him—well, not that it was even pompousness, he just plain annoyed me, and it made it worse that I almost hoped I'd see him again, today.

I climbed the steps to the second floor and surveyed the area quickly before moving past the assortment of tables and chairs to the bookshelves. I didn't plan to mindlessly wander this time, I prepared myself.

In the little bit of time my mother allowed me to use her laptop, I scoured the library's website in search of an adventure—well, a literary adventure, because at this point in my life, I wasn't searching for a real one.

I liked comfort and security. It was nice having a plan compete with bullet points and well-organized notes. So, naturally, I was the kind of person whose adventures came from documentaries on the History Channel. I would sit all day admiring the tragedy of the World Wars with my cat, Luis, snuggled in my lap.

However, since I discovered the "real" story of Atlantis in The Lost City, I realized I was in a greater state of wanderlust than I thought, and the only way to cure it was to take my mind somewhere else. I thought maybe I'd search for Pompeii before the wanderlust grew too strong and I did the unwise thing of choosing want before need.

I rounded a row of books and stepped down a new aisle, eyes searching for something of interest. I was just plucking a compact book from the top shelf when a face came level with mine from one aisle over, eyes smiling at me from between a gap in the bookshelf.

"Was it mesmeric?" Asked the face.

I jumped a little, nearly dropping the book I'd just picked out. The word choice and high nose were telltale signs of the strange librarian from the other day. A strange mix of dread and excitement brewed in my gut when I recognized him.

He laughed quietly and whispered an apology. Then, suddenly, he was wheeling the book cart into my aisle.

"You're Jovie, right?"

I was startled to hear my name from him since we hadn't exchanged names before. My brows furrowed in confusion and his expectant expression turned bashful.

"Oh, I searched the registry to see if you ended up checking it out. Wasn't hard. I was the last person to check it out before you—it was you, wasn't it?"

My eyes narrowed while my lips twitched in disbelief. "You checked the registry…"

He put his hands up in defense, and quickly began a chorus of "no's". "I wasn't being creepy," he claimed, hands waving frantically, "I just didn't want to embarrass myself by asking about the book if you didn't read it…"He paused and pinched the bridge of his nose between his fingers.. "Not that I haven't just embarrassed myself now…" His face turned blotchy and he lifted a book from the cart to hide his face behind. "I am so sorry."

I pressed my lips together, trying hard not to laugh, but failing when I couldn't hold back the grin that threatened to appear. There was nothing eloquent about his blundering—and the image he had tried so hard to create the other day just crumbled before him in a string of garbled stutters.

I decided to mock him a little.

"It truly was mesmeric," I told him past a light chuckle. "In fact, I found the storyline to be quite prodigious."

His eyes slowly appeared over the top of the book in his hands. "You liked it?" The stutter seemed to disappear and light inquisition returned to his voice. My lips pursed at the shift in confidence. He had a funny way of carrying himself.

"I guess."

He lowered the book completely and tucked a piece of hair behind his ear. I decided I didn't much care for his shoulder length locks. The longer I looked at him, the more alien-like he appeared.

Suddenly, he knelt down beside the cart and ran an index finger over the spines of the books stashed there.

I glanced down the aisle, unsure of what to do. I decided to scan the book I picked out, but realized shortly that I didn't want it and put it back on the shelf. All the while the strange librarian hummed to himself, searching for who-knows-what. I questioned whether or not to walk away.

"Drat," he muttered after what felt like forever. "It's not here. Figures. If you thought The Lost City was enthralling, you'd love Meryl Island."

I grimaced. "A story about an island? Those are always creepy."

"It's completely disturbing. You have to read it."

There was an excited gleam in his eye and I felt my insides warm. The interest he seemed to take in me came out of nowhere, and it made me nervous because I didn't know what to expect. I didn't make friends easily. Besides, I wasn't one to take suggestions from people—he got lucky the first time.

I began to shake my head, but he nodded in response. "I have incredible taste in literature."

He had fierce light blue eyes that dared me to take him up on his offer and prove him wrong.

I looked over at the bookshelf beside us, thinking about the kind of adventure I really came searching for, and when my eyes met his again, I knew I was going to give in.

With a sigh, I answered, "Okay."

The corners of his lips turned up and then he turned the cart around. I took a step toward him and his hand shot out. "I'm Bash, by the way."

Cautiously, I put my hand in his and he gave it a firm squeeze.

"Bash?" I questioned.

"Sebastian Daley the Third, actually," he quipped. "Just imagine Christmas at my parent's humble abode. Three Sebastians'." He shook his head at the sheer ridiculousness. "So, I started calling myself Bash. Things got far less confusing after that."

He lead me across the library in silence for a few strides before talking, again. "Jovie, then?"

I nodded.

"A form of jovial. It means happy, cheerful, jubilant." His elbow nudged my arm lightly. "Your parents must have been excited to have you."

I snorted, lips contorting into goofy excuse for a frown, mostly because I just wanted to laugh. "My mom is the mayor," I said.

Nearly everyone in town knew about the relationship between my mother and her secretary. It was the closest thing Ashwood Creek ever got to a scandal. Sure, Mayor Sinclair seemed practically perfect in every way, but could anyone ever let her live down her one mistake? Guess again.

"That doesn't mean anything to me. I'm not from here," Bash told me.

I lifted my eyebrows and clasped my hands together. "Oh," I said. "Well, it's just a little ironic."

"I won't ask."

"Thanks," I said, quietly.

We came to a shelf on the opposite side of the library. Nobody else was near us and it was the one place in the library that didn't have windows. The genre on the plaque above the books read "Nonfiction: Horror."

My eyes grew. Bash noticed and chuckled. "Ominous but fascinating. Trust me on this."

The wheels of the cart squeaked as he slowed it to a stop. Without even having to examine the shelf, Bash pulled out the second book from the top right. It was thin and black with bold white lettering.

"Tell me how you like it," he offered with a smile.

That weekend, as always, I went to Henry's.

I loved my father, admired him, really, but the weekends were always somewhat uncomfortable. He had a tiny little shoebox of an apartment with one bedroom—so, I slept on the pull out couch. Another thing, they didn't allow pets, so I couldn't bring Luis with.

Now, it's not like I didn't enjoy spending time with my father because of the living arrangements, because I did, it's just that, in my eyes, he was a strange man.

Henry was excitable and witty. More times than not, he insisted we treat each other as friends instead of family.

In the mornings we made breakfast together. At night, we'd watch the History Channel until one of us began to snore. He had weird things all over his house—art things from when he was in high school. A painting of an eye greeted guests at the door, a failed life-size dog sculpture stood next to the couch, and he had a collection of ceramic bowls placed around the house even though they served no purpose.

If my mother introduced me to this man for the first time that day and told me he was my father, I wouldn't believe her. He was too "out there", not something my mother would ever consider procreating with. But, she did, and I'm living proof of it.

At my mother's house, everything had a place. We didn't have useless things lying about the house—not like Henry's sculptures. We had family pictures, area rugs, plants—but that's as crazy as we got. My mother liked blue, so everything in the house had a color scheme of blues, greys, and whites.

Henry's home on the other hand? There probably wasn't a single matching furniture item in his entire apartment.

So, after spending all week with my put-together mother, it's no wonder I thought my own father was bizarre.

My mother walked me up to Henry's floor, carrying my suitcase for me even though she was still wearing her work heels. When I tried to take it from her, she swatted my hand away and told me "I've got it." As we walked, she did what she always does: place her hand on the small of my back as if she were guiding me.

Henry had a red door, and when we reached it, I knocked. My mother let out a sigh beside me and set my suitcase down. Henry opened up a moment later.

Behind the frame of his glasses, he observed me first with a smile, "Hey, Jo-Jo."

"Hey," I said. I was, admittedly, a little winded from the walk up the stairs, and the heat got worse every day in Ashwood Creek. I started to fan myself with my hand.

He turned to my mother. "Hello, Mer."

My mother blinked a couple of times and smoothed down the front of her blouse. "Henry, we are professionals, I am your boss. To you, I am Ms. Sinclair or Meredith."

Henry rolled his eyes. "It's been nearly eighteen years--"

My mother waved a hand at him and then turned to me.

"Have fun, I'll see you Monday."

She pressed a short kiss into my hair and then hurried back down the hall.

I sighed and turned toward Henry, used to how uncomfortable their interactions were, but also a little tired with their awkwardness.

Henry stuffed his hands in his pockets and kept his eyes steady on her even after she disappeared down the stairwell.

In an effort to lighten the mood, he smiled mischievously and muttered to me, "She had no objections to 'Mer' the night you were conceived."

My eyes widened in alarm while my cheeks flushed. I grabbed my suitcase and lifted it into the apartment, pushing past him. "Oh my god, Henry. I did not need to know that."

"It's true," he sang after me while I heaved my suitcase toward the couch.

I had Meryl Island, which I planned to finish over the weekend, in my other hand. Only a chapter in and I was already questioning the reality of my entire life. Bash was right. It was so disturbing it was fascinating.

I heard the front door close and Henry popped up beside me a second later. "Put in a good word for me," he advised while ruffling his greying curls.

I lifted an eyebrow and dropped down onto the couch. "She pretty much avoids any kind of relationship."

Henry shrugged. "I know," he said. Then, he sat down next to me with a little groan. "She's got to be real lonely."

I opened Meryl's Island and lifted my feet, crossing them under me on the cushions. "I don't know. I think being alone is just who she is."

I never thought my mom was unhappy, or rather, I knew she wasn't. I knew because I was just like her and I wasn't unhappy living my life the way I did.

My mom wasn't a relationship person, but that doesn't mean she didn't like people. She liked people. Of course she did, she was the mayor. She prided herself in making things a little better for everyone. That's all she ever felt she needed to do. That's the kind of love she believed in. Romantic love was a want, and it's something she just deemed unnecessary.

I got that, but I also got Henry.

Henry didn't understand how someone couldn't want that kind of love, romantic love. To him, finding romantic love was part of life. Just like people have to go through puberty, they have to feel romantic love.

I got that, but I didn't think it was true. You don't have to fall in love. Really, you don't. It's a choice, and a beautiful one at that.

You know what it all comes down to? It comes down to a couple of questions: Do I want to be with this person? Do I trust them? Do they make me happy?

If you ever say "I need them," you're never going to be happy.

I think that's what's wrong with Henry's perspective. He convinced himself he needed my mother's love, and because of that he's stuck. If he just told himself he didn't need it, he'd be free.

"Well," Henry says, "don't let that dictate who you are." I glanced up from my book and he wrapped an arm around my shoulders. "You've got one life. Every couple miles, go down a path you wouldn't normally take. You're a smart girl, navigation should be easy."

And so, here Henry helped me make a future decision. He was right, I already knew the difference between need and want—but applying them both to my life at the same time? That's something I hadn't done yet.

Chapter 3

I started to spend much more time at the library. As soon as I finished one book, Bash would hand me another. I picked out a spot in the library, my spot where Bash could always find me. It was in the corner of the biography section, beside a window that overlooked the park. I sat and read until closing time, and Bash would stop by to take any finished book I had and replace it with another.

He read everything: comedies, nonfiction, horror, history, romance, adventure, sci-fi. Titles like: Ford Rucker's Guide to Staying Alive, Pendulum, Tragedy on Seventh Street, Verona's Very Bad Idea, Twelve Missed Kisses.

He found books I've never heard of in every kind of condition. Old, new, falling apart, never-been-opened, coffee stained, dogged eared pages, crisp, right off the press paper.

He had the place wired, and he snaked around the aisles so quietly you'd never know he existed. Sometimes I questioned if he was real or if I had hallucinated him in the overheated state I was in upon meeting him. One second you may look up from your book and be surrounded by nothingness, the next he'd be standing over your shoulder checking what page you were on.

On this day in particular, he was late to bring me a new book, so I slouched back in the leather cushions of the library chair I claimed and stared out at the park. Twelve Missed Kisses rested on the corner of my knee, waiting to be snatched.

I thought about the look on Quinn's face when I told her I didn't want to go to the waterpark again today. She was mad that I kept blowing her off, and with the reputation I had with friendships, I guess I couldn't blame her. She probably thought she hit her expiration date—which wasn't true—I was just tired of tanning lotion and bikinis and endless babbling about boys. If I left my fate in her hands, she'd have me on a hundred blind dates by the end of summer.

"What did you think?"

It had been a couple of weeks since our first meeting, and he always asked the same question when he greeted me. Bash's voice was something I could recognize easily by now. It was low and soft, and his words always sounded slurred together. I didn't know where he was from, but the more I listened to him talk, the more distinct the dialect difference became.

I turned my eyes away from the park to look at him. He had his hair swept back in a ponytail again, and he wore a plain colored short-sleeve button up and slacks. Today, he abandoned the book cart and sat down in the chair next to mine, separated only by a low side table.

I lifted the book and offered it to him, which he accepted and then looked at me expectantly.

"Not your best pick," I advised him.

His mouth dropped open in a scoff. "What are you, some kind of grouch? Remy and Ferra are charming, and their love story is refreshing. By the end you yearn for something as wonderful as what they had."

I shrugged and slapped my hands on my knees somewhat defeatedly, because this is how he reacted every time I told him I didn't care for one of his stories. "It's corny."

"Of course it's corny," Bash squabbles, "Romance is corny. That's the whole point. It's supposed to make you feel silly."

I exhaled deeply and shook my head.

His eyes narrowed, lips pinching together. "I think you just like to argue for arguments sake."

While his statement was somewhat true, it wasn't true at that moment. I sat up, crossing my arms. "Oh, c'mon, you can do better than that."

"I could," he agreed. "I've got a better selection of books at my place. You would never believe how many fantastic books this place is missing."

"Given your taste in books..."

"Hey!" He pointed to me accusingly. It took some effort to keep a straight face, especially the more he got flustered.

"Don't you have some books to be shelving?" I asked. This is the longest he'd hung around. Usually, he'd drop a new book in my lap, ask how I liked the other one, and move on. He normally didn't make himself comfortable in the chair across from me.

"Always," he sighed, "but I've got time."

I raised an eyebrow, and when he made eye contact, cleared my throat and looked back out the window. He must have sensed I wasn't interested in discussing anything other than books because he scooted forward and got up. I kept my gaze on the park until another book was set in my lap.

"Let me know what you think, Jovial."

"Jovie—"

He laughed. "I know. Just for jocularity."

He had found out I thought his word choice was, at times, ridiculous. The corners of my lips turned up softly, and my eyes followed him until he disappeared the way he always does, in a blink.

The more time I spent there, the better Bash and I came to know each other. Sometimes, he would abandon his book cart for twenty minutes or more so that he could sit and chat books with me. Every once in a while he craftily turned the conversation elsewhere and we learned some things about each other.

He was twenty, and transferred to Ashwood Creek from L.A. where he said the bustle became overwhelming. He liked it here where things were sleepy and he could hear himself think. He liked big words and loud music. When he got embarrassed he covered his face as if that would trick me into thinking he wasn't blushing. He had two older sisters. He hated when I called him Sebastian. "That's my father's name," he would say. "Also, my grandfather's."

What he learned about me was not to the same extent as him. I was more reserved, and he didn't seem to mind. I thought he would feel weird about me being seventeen, but when I told him it appeared not to faze him. He called me a nerd for watching the History Channel, which was ironic because he's the one who apparently had five hundred and twelve books lying around his apartment. He already knew I was the mayor's daughter, but when he learned my last name was not hers, he didn't ask any more questions. I liked that about him, he wasn't unbearably nosey. He was able to sense when to change the subject or go back to book stacking.

A month after I met him, he left his phone number in a sticky note on the inside cover of a book called The Domino Effect.

Under his number was a message:

I am not hitting on you—but I think we could use some time away from the library. Call me if you'd consider being friends.

—Bash

P.S. The other librarians tease me about you. Help.

Dinner with my mother was usually quiet. We would cook together, and then sit down to eat. She did most of her talking while we were bustling around the kitchen, reaching over each other, running tap water, and pulling cabinet doors open. After that, we usually had all of our conversation in, and the night would fade into silence.

Tonight, however, my mother wanted to talk through dinner.

"What did you do today while I was working?"

She had already asked that, but I repeated my answer. "Just lazed around reading."

She spooned some green beans onto her plate and raised an eyebrow. I stopped cutting my chicken, brows furrowing. "What?"

"Mrs. Alberstein told me you weren't talking to Quinn anymore?"

"Not true." I sighed.

"Also, you've been leaving the neighborhood?"

There was a stack of books at the end of the dinner table, I had set them there when I got home and pointed to them now. "Reading," I repeated. "Been going to the library."

"You should take Quinn."

I snorted. "Quinn at a library? Laughing, I shook my head. "Mom, she's just fine shopping and hanging out at the waterpark with Zoey and Noel. You know that's not my thing. I always feel like an outsider, anyway."

"You're not an outsider to Quinn."

I knew I wasn't an outsider to Quinn. I was an outsider to the rest of her friends, though. They only hung out with me because I was friends with Quinn. Besides, I had a new routine, and I liked it. Then, there was Bash who might think he scared me off if I didn't return. I didn't mind him so much and I didn't want to give him the impression that I did. Maybe I would call him, just to let him know that.

"Fine," I said. "I'll hang out with her tomorrow."

"Okay," she replied, and swung back into her normal routine. Everything that needed to be said was said, and we left ourselves to the silence.

That night after getting ready for bed, I crawled into bed next to Luis, who was purring on my pillow, and grabbed my phone off the nightstand. The books from the library were now at the foot of my bed. I opened up The Domino Effect and plucked the sticky note from the inside cover.

I had my doubts. I wasn't a very good friend. When I got bored of people, or felt like there was too much effort involved in maintaining the friendship, I didn't hang on to them. I let them go, stopped putting in the effort, and stopped communicating. It was one of the worse habits that I picked up from my mother.

So far, things were easy with Bash. I figured if he wanted to be friends, we could try. I'd just warn him, first.

I ran a hand through my hair and began to dial Bash's number. I could feel my pulse quicken out of nervousness. As I listened to the dial tone, my mind went blank. What would I say?

"Hello?"

It was Bash's voice. Low and slurred.

"Hey, it's Jovie."

"Does this mean you've considered a friendship?" There was a sense of humor in his voice, and I liked it. I thought he had the kind of voice that could calm a storm or encourage world peace. The kind of voice you'd like to fall asleep listening to. It put me at ease. I hadn't noticed that before, and maybe it was because I was so focused on his face.

I let out the breath I had been holding. "Yeah, listen," I said.

"Okay," he said softly.

I struggled, trying to find the right way to say how I felt about initiating this friendship. My hand found Luis, and I began to absently stroke his tabby fur.

"Look, Bash," I began, "I'm kind of like a spinning wheel. I can't have anything in my life that will slow me down and cause me to teeter and fall over. I just need you to know that before you make the mistake of thinking you can trust me."

There was a short moment of silence on the other end, and I wondered if he had hung up, just like I would have done if I were him. I understood how frustrating I could be, but I didn't want to change myself, I just pitied the people who got to know me.

"I can let go as easily as I can hold on," he replied. "Just tell me when."

If only we knew how much this would hurt in the end.

Chapter 4

Quinn Alberstein was the kind of girl that really liked being a teenager. She liked crushes, and friends she thought would last forever, makeup, shopping with her parent's cash, experimenting, and above all: gossip—but not the kind of gossip that lands you the title Queen Bee. She just liked to talk.

Through this, she gained the knowledge about nearly everyone important and unimportant in both school and town. But, she wasn't the type to spread rumors. She knew there were very few people she could trust to share all of these things with, and I happened to be one of them.

I was the perfect person for a chatty girl to spill the secrets of a hundred teenagers to.

Why?

I simply didn't care.

I'd zone out, forget, lose complete interest.

I didn't care if Walt Hamilton was in the closet, or whether or not Rumor Jackson gained a few pounds. I was the perfect place to take rumors to die. I was perfect because I was too busy trying to cover up my own personal life to care about anyone else.

Being friends with Quinn became increasingly difficult as we aged. She had to know everything about me. She was one of those people. I didn't like those people, but I put up with her because she'd been in my life for such a long time that I couldn't just tell her goodbye and never see her again.

We'd been best friends since we were babies. She had an idea of how I operated—but that didn't mean she didn't slip what she considered "unimportant" information about me to her other friends, because she did from time to time.

Information we found important about ourselves differed entirely.

For example, if I told her about my friendship with Bash, she would immediately jump to the conclusion that we were trying to "get it on". Next thing I'd know, Zoey and Noel would be asking questions about a boyfriend I didn't even have. I couldn't have that getting around. I couldn't lie. But, even if I told the truth, nobody would believe me.

Hiding my personal life was tough job in high school. Having a friend like Quinn made it a little harder. She was insanely intuitive.

"Something's different."

I glanced over at the lawn chair beside me. Quinn was relaxed across it, legs up, sunglasses down. She had a magazine in her lap and lipgloss in the cup holder. We were on her front lawn in bikini tops and shorts, letting the sun tan our skin. Just a couple houses down the chickens were squawking. You could hear the faint hum of the Pea Shucker's voice as he sang show tunes.

I pushed my sunglasses up into my hair and closed a newly recommended book from Bash on my finger to hold my page. I'd seen him once since our phone call. Then, I had to make plans with Quinn, as promised.

She reached over and wrapped a finger around a lock of my short dark hair, pursing her lips.

"I think the sun's lightening your hair."

I couldn't see that being possible. Since our waterpark escapades, I spent most of my time inside reading. We'd only been outside for an hour and a half.

"Right," I said, letting the tone of my voice reflect my disbelief.

"Really," she assured me with a half grin and pulled her hand back into her lap. "So..." She snapped her magazine shut and sat up. "Where have you been going—because it hasn't been to the waterpark with me and the girls."

I flipped my sunglasses back down to mask an eye roll. I didn't understand why my business was so important. Lifting the book, I pointed to the cover.

"Library."

One of her dirty blonde eyebrows rose and she bit her lip mischievously. "What's at the library?" Her voice rose curiously. It was painfully obvious as to what she was suggesting.

I laughed at her and shook my head. "Books, Quinn. Just books."

"Well, you've never seemed this...interested."

Scoffing, I shook my head again and slouched back into the lawn chair, making like I was going to read again.

Quinn reached over and snatched the book, which nearly made me turn over the lawn chair when I scrambled to grab it back.

"Lucifer's Revenge," she read and then looked up at me in shock, her mouth so wide I thought she might break her jaw. "Oh my God, are you joining a cult?"

"What? No! It's fiction," I explained as I, again, reached to claim the book.

I thought about how normally I would have let her take it. I would have been mature and crossed my arms until she got bored and tossed it back. This was different, though. I almost felt possessive.

She dropped the book in my lap like it was a snake or her dad's dirty underwear. "I'm going to believe you're in a cult unless you tell me why you spend so much time at the library."

It's the kind of thing she'd joke about with Zoey and Noel. I was weird enough, I didn't need everyone thinking I worshiped Satan. Then again, I didn't want Quinn to tease me about Bash. My safety was the books, but she wasn't buying it.

I made a frustrated noise in the back of my throat, which only confirmed that I was, in fact, trying to hide something from her; because like a dog's ears perk up when they hear the word "walk", her head tilted a little to the right and she removed her sunglasses. Her green eyes sparkled.

There was only one way to save myself. Turn Bash into something unappealing.

"I'm friends with a librarian there," I said, cringing at the way it sounded.

Now I was the girl who watched History Channel, stayed in with her cat, and made friends with librarians. I wasn't dumb. I knew social suicide when I saw it. I cared a lot about how people saw me. I only wished they'd lack interest in me the same way I lacked interest in them.

"You're kidding."

I shook my head. This was better than relentless prodding into my love life, the complete tearing of the curtain between personal and social life.

"Please come to the waterpark with us tomorrow." She had this concerned look on her face I'm not sure I'd ever seen take form before. It was almost as bad as the look on my mother's face whenever I told her I cut a friend loose. For being a woman who did that a lot herself, you'd think she'd feel indifferent about it.

I sighed and pushed my hair up off my neck. The heat was only frustrating me more. The more she insisted, the more I wanted to escape.

"Quinn..."

"A librarian friend on top of satanic book choices." She shook her head. "Jovie, I'm not going to lie here, you're worrying me."

I groaned and flipped my legs over the side of the lawn chair, sitting up. "Oh, just because I don't spend all day gawking at boys and educating myself on the people in Ashwood

Creek doesn't mean I'm crazy. It's just boring. Everything about it feels ridiculous."

Her eyebrows furrowed together. She didn't seem insulted, but she wasn't exactly happy with me either. "God, sometimes you're so pretentious." Her voice had a bite. "You're not any better than me because you've functioned like a human algorithm machine since preschool."

I squeezed my eyes shut and let out a breath. "Quinn, that's not what I was saying—"

"Good grief," she continued as she stood up. "Take a break from your mommy issues and live a little."

Something in me snapped, and I jerked away from Quinn's hand when she tried to put a hand on my shoulder. "Excuse me?"

Her eyebrows pinched together. "What?"

"Mommy issues?" The words left a bad taste in my mouth.

She let out an exaggerated groan and rolled her eyes. "C'mon, Jovie. Your desperate search for perfection and order stems from some unresolved issues with your mom—like everything you do is for her approval. I've known you my whole life. It's not hard to miss. You've made her your identity. Jo."

I gripped the side of the lawn chair so hard my knuckles turned white. "I don't want to go to the waterpark," I said as I grabbed my book and stood.

"Where are you going?" Quinn's voice followed me as I turned and walked toward the sidewalk, away from her house.

"Home," I called back. "I'll see you later."

"Jovie!"

My resentment broke forth from their chains when I tossed a bitter look over my shoulder and said, "I've got mommy issues to sort out."

She was right and I was ashamed. It was something I didn't like thinking about, something I hoped people wouldn't notice about me.

I avoided Quinn for a little while after that, too embarrassed and too guarded to discuss it. Walking away from things was something I had perfected over the years. I was very good at it.

I met Bash outside the library for the first time a couple days after the incident with Quinn. It was strange seeing him in something other than button downs and khakis and without his trusty sidekick: the book cart. I'd gotten so used to seeing him as part of the library that removing him from that place made him intimidating. Suddenly, I didn't know who he was.

We rendezvoused at the park beside the library, a location in town both of us were familiar with. I remember being nervous. It was unlike me to meet up with anyone other than Quinn. But, after what Quinn said days before, it made me think perhaps it wasn't unlike me. Perhaps it was unlike my mother. Somehow, it made me feel a little more confident about meeting Bash that day.

I rode my bike there which left my short hair windswept. Yet, the breeze wasn't enough to fight the heat. He was waiting on one of the many small walk bridges that crossed a creek running through the park. His hair was pulled back into a ponytail and his eyes shielded by a pair of aviator sunglasses. When he saw me near the bridge he smiled brightly.

"You look radiant!" He called out to me.

It was a silly thing to call me, really. My hair was a mess and I didn't dress up for him. I was just me in a tank top and shorts, sweating in the humidity. I wouldn't call that radiant, but the compliment still had its desired effect.

I shook my head but goosebumps surfaced on my skin and my lips turned up. He had a way of making me feel like I had just drunk ice water—my throat felt tight, yet there was a feeling of odd satisfaction.

"What is it you want?" I asked as I came to stand beside him, unsure of how to approach him now. Usually he smelled like dusty books and linen, but not this time. The proximity revealed a musky amber scent with detergent undertones and the faintest trace of tobacco. It was like meeting him for the first time.

"Just to see you, Jovial." His voice was light. His forearms rested on the railing and I placed a hand beside them.

"Cute," I said and scrunched my nose.

"I like it when you do that," he said, tapping his own nose.

The goosebumps reappeared, so I tucked my hair behind my ear and crossed my arms. "You're weird."

He shrugged and then straightened and turned to lean against the railing with his backside. "I thought I might invite you on an adventure. You seem as though you need one."

I scoffed and turned to lean with him. "Oh, really?"

He laughed a little. "How do you feel about catching a bus into Winsor tomorrow morning? See a couple bands perform at a music festival?"

My eyes grew at the request and I got a nervous feeling in the pit of my stomach. My first instinct was to say no. How could I "catch a bus" with a person I barely knew? It was wildly irresponsible, and I couldn't give him an answer without getting permission first. I felt like a child, and that alone made me feel inadequate enough to find a way out of it. It was absurd to even consider.

"Uh, sorry," I began, fingers clenching tight onto my arm and eyes focusing hard on a tree a couple of yards away. "I don't think that's possible for me."

"We could be back at any time," he told me. "Winsor is only an hour from here. If you need to be back before some-time—I'm not saying we, you know, get tangled up in any trouble—just listen to music. Dance maybe. I'd just really love to...get better acquainted."

He removed his sunglasses halfway through his speech and hung them on his shirt. He now looked at me with a sincere gaze, blue eyes trying convince and reassure. He was someone you felt like you could never say no to. There was something about him that made me want to break all of my personal rules, to upset the balance. I'd never met someone as intoxicatingly genuine as him. It was dangerous, but I felt myself cracking.

Tomorrow was a Friday. My mother would be working until seven. Maybe she didn't have to know. Maybe nobody did and it could be my secret. I'd never done anything like that before, my mind was buzzing with the possibility.

I was so conflicted knowing that the right thing to do was to accept that I couldn't go. But, what was there for me in Ashwood Creek right now?

Nothing.

Was it really upsetting the balance? It was summer. Everything would turn slowly until the school year started, again. Maybe I could afford to do something out of the ordinary.

This wasn't like me, but my mother never had to find out. If she didn't find out, I could do anything. I had no obligations. I could say yes.

"I hate to put you in a state of ambivalence," Bash said after things had been silent between us for some time. Only the sound of the creek and rustling leaves kept my mind from floating away before he said something and brought me back to the ground.

"I…" My mind was still clouded. "What time does the bus leave?"

"Nine."

I nodded to myself, thinking that my mother left at eight thirty every morning without fail. That gave me enough time to bike to the bus station.

My stomach was in knotted, but my mind was made up. "I'll see you then."

Chapter 5

When I woke up the following morning, I had a bad feeling in the pit of my stomach. It was a feeling that told me I should ditch, call Bash and tell him to go without me. But, when that thought crossed my mind, all I could think about was Henry and Quinn, what they said about me—my mother.

I lived by the motto: What would mom do?

Henry was right. I couldn't let that dictate my life. Maybe like Quinn said, I did need to "live a little." Right now, I had everything I needed. I could take that road less traveled by if I wanted to. I was smart enough to know when to cut things off. I was good at that. I could do this. Besides, Bash made me feel like I could be exactly who I was. He made me feel comfortable enough to make a decision I normally wouldn't.

I didn't know him, he didn't know me. We could be anything we wanted together. This was my fork in the road. I didn't need to take it, but, God, I wanted to.

I silently got ready while my mother did and then got back under the covers to wait for her to leave. Usually, I was a late sleeper. If she caught me awake, she'd spend time asking questions I couldn't answer. I felt like a disappointment if I wasn't honest. I had to avoid her in order to make sneaking away for the day easier.

She came to check on me before she left, but with my face tilted away she couldn't see my closed eyes were twitching—a dead giveaway that I was a fake. Although I knew she wouldn't react as dramatically as I was playing it up, I couldn't have any loose ends.

The second my door close, I sat up and threw my bed sheets off. I heard her car start, and by then my feet were already stuffed in my shoes and purse tossed over my shoulder.

I waited three minutes for her to drive down the street before pulling open the front door and darting down the driveway toward my bike. The Pea Shucker wasn't out yet, but the chickens began to scream. I figured the neighborhood was too sleepy to notice but still hurried away, their chatter following me to the end of the block.

The morning was cool, and the sky a little grey. When I arrived at the bus station, Bash was waiting with our tickets. Despite the clouds he wore a brimmed hat and sunglasses. His tank top was black and had giant white letters on it that I couldn't make out. When he saw me, he offered two thumbs up and jogged over to the bike rack where I was locking up.

"Bus leaves in five," he told me and pointed at a bus that looked ready to go but was still semi-empty. It wasn't a surprise, considering the times; still, it made my numbed nerves come back to life.

I stood up straight after securing my bike and followed him. "Why don't we take a car?" I asked.

He cleared his throat and pointed over his shoulder. "See that red bike beside yours? That's mine. I don't have a car. See, I moved here from L.A., share an apartment, and work in a library all while drowning in university debt. I can barely afford groceries much less a couple gallons of gas."

"Oh," I said, embarrassed to have even asked.

He jabbed an elbow at my arm and grinned. "Don't feel bad. It's fun to explore my other options."

I followed him onto the bus where he handed off our tickets to the driver and then lead me back to a row of empty seats. He pocketed the return tickets as he sat, then reached over me and unhooked the blinds so that he could see out the window.

"Nervous?" He asked after removing his hat and sunglasses and set them on the floor beside our feet.

I twisted my hands together in my lap and nodded.

"It'll be fun," he reassured me. Reaching over, he placed a hand over mine and squeezed. "I promise."

My fingers twisted nervously in my lap as I looked out the bus window at the passing trees. We were somewhere in the country now, a clty out from Ashwood Creek. Bash sat beside me, looking over my shoulder with vague interest. For the past twenty minutes we had been listening to the couple sitting behind us chat about dysfunctional distant family, but they had since dozed off.

It wasn't uncomfortable silence between Bash and I, but I desperately wanted there to be words to fill the void. I didn't have second thoughts, but my mind would only dwell on all of the rules I was breaking if it didn't stay distracted.

Bash's arm brushed against mine and then nudged my arm away so he could steal my armrest.

My lips pursed and I glanced sideways to find him waiting with playful grin. He licked his lips when I noticed him and then leaned in.

"I forgot to tell you earlier," he began, the smile he wore shining in his voice. "You look entrancing."

His breath batted against my skin, words tangling in my hair and encouraging a light blush to flood my face. I hated that he did that to me. He knew how I felt about long-lasting friendships or any kind of commitment. It scared me to death and I always rationalized my way out of it. He was such a romantic—which I figured must have been because of all those books.

"It sounds so fake when you say things like that: entrancing, radiant..." I muttered, even though my lips had turned up in a soft smile.

He huffed. "Fake?" He asked. "You know what's fake? The word 'beautiful'." He shook his head as though just saying the word offended him. "Why would I call you something as tired as that? Nearly every girl gets called beautiful in her life—and why? There are so many other words to flatter women with—so many better words to capture the feelings they evoke."

A sudden rush of admiration flooded my system. It felt like I was weighted down by a thousand bricks or melted into the bus seats. His voice was like slow-melting chocolate in the hot sun, and paired with those words was like finding a caramel drizzle—smooth and sweet. A part of me found it funny that a couple of pretty words could make me feel that way, but he gazed at me like I was every word beautiful could not describe.

"Why aren't you afraid of me?" I asked. "You seem like the kind of person that devotes their whole heart to someone. I'm the kind of person that will drop off the face of the earth when I've had enough. Isn't it destructive being as open as you are with someone like me?"

He pinched his lips between his fingers and thought about it for a moment. Hardly any time passed before he shrugged and answered me.

"I'm not going to say life is too short—because that's a lie. Life is the longest thing any of us will ever experience. I also won't say I have no regrets, because I have too many to count. Usually, I just ask myself 'why not?' and that's the end of the argument. What's a life without experience?"

I didn't know what to say, because 'why not?' never seemed good enough for me. He was organized chaos, and I just didn't get it.

"Why put yourself through all of that, though?"

Again, he shrugged. "Life would be so boring without fears and heartbreak and confusion. I want to feel everything, see everything, and be anything."

"You're so lucky," I sighed. Just thinking about experiencing everything he wanted to was overwhelming.

"What's your philosophy, then?" He asked inquiringly. He leaned back in his seat as though getting comfortable for a long explanation.

I exhaled and rocked my head back against the headrest. To me, life was more complicated than a couple of reckless choices designed to make me feel something. All I could see were flaws and regret. I wanted to minimize hardships, take any and all preventative measures.

"Life isn't a whiteboard," I explained. "You can't just scribble haphazardly across the board and erase it all when you decide you don't like it anymore. You draw with a permanent marker; you're careful about where you put that cloud and how big the petals of the flower are. There's no going back, no erasing. You live with the mistakes you make. I don't want to hate the final product, you know?"

He tapped his fingers on his knees thoughtfully, nodding slowly as he considered what I said.

"How about this," he finally spoke, "I'll be Picasso, you be da Vinci."

We smiled at each other. "Deal," I agreed.

I guess he had a point. Two vastly different artists can be successful. To some, realism is the finest art, but to others, a little chaos is a masterpiece. Either way, they're both beautiful.

Satisfied, Picasso removed his forearm from my armrest and settled back into silence. I rolled my head toward him and watched the sunlight catch his blonde eyelashes and reflect in those wide eyes of his. My insides were doing somersaults, and I couldn't control the goosebumps that were popping up along my skin.

It's crazy how you've always been one thing and then suddenly you meet someone, or hear something, and you think about being something different—even if the only difference is believing you can do something you normally thought you couldn't.

Winsor was a fairly big city with a giant city square that hosted a music festival every summer. Bands from all around would gather and play music for half-drunk spectators that threw their hands in the hair and rocked their sweaty, sun kissed bodies to the beat of the songs.

When Bash and I stepped off the bus, we had to walk half a block up the mostly packed square. People were filling in quickly, some with lawn chairs on the outer corners, but others squeezed together at the front of a makeshift stage. It was pretty crowded, so I was both relieved and stunned when Bash grabbed my hand, lacing his fingers in between mine. I knew he did it so that we wouldn't lose each other, but the hiccup my heart made was undeniable.

I couldn't believe he made me feel this way. The last time this happened I was in elementary school crushing on the flag-football quarterback. It absolutely didn't count and I'd dismissed every other feeling a boy might have given me until now. Usually, by now I would have bored potential suitors away, but Bash held true, and it was both exciting and nerve-wracking.

I didn't know whether to shy away or encourage him. Shying away is something my mother would do, so I decided to reject it—especially now while I was away doing something she would disapprove of. So, I squeezed his hand.

All I had to do was remind myself of summer and all the time I had to pretend I wasn't what I was, and I could do anything.

We stepped into the densely pack crowd of spectators both young and old. Bash stuck his sunglasses back on and pulled down the brim of his hat to shade his face, then he pulled me across his body so that I stood in front of him. I felt lost in crowd without being able to see or touch him, totally disconnected from the only person I knew. So, I leant back so that his chest pressed against my back and he wrapped his arms around my shoulders to reassure me of his presence.

When I got used to the stimulus of my surroundings, I could finally hear the music. In that moment I felt so free, so far away from everything that I was. Bash and I rocked slowly from side to side, and I closed my eyes.

In my mind, shackles cracked open and I wandered out of my self-appointed cell into the sunlight. It burned my skin and blinded me, so that when I looked in the mirror, I couldn't even recognize myself.

It felt so safe in secure in his arms. I thought I could live in that moment forever with my back flush against his chest, so much that I could feel our hearts pulse together to the beat of the drums. I think it was then that I began to fall in love.

Bash was going to be my crooked cloud in the painting of my life if things didn't work out, and I'm sure da Vinci had a slip-up somewhere, too.

This was my short moment of pure bliss, a moment where I was nothing but me—completely and entirely me: a little timid and falling fast in a hazy cloud of uncertainty. I wanted this so bad, more than I ever wanted anything before. It was raw desire, a splurge in the most human direction of my life. No robotics, no logic—I couldn't even rationalize anymore. I was dizzy and spinning, knowing there were chemical reactions I couldn't even fathom happening in the deepest corners of my brain.

It was entirely dangerous, stupid really, but I knew if he asked me to jump, I would—knowing that when I fell, I would land in his arms.

It was so early, we hardly knew each other, but I was a spinning wheel, and I didn't want thinking to slow me down.

We were sun kissed and smiling when we arrived back in Ashwood Creek. He held my hand the whole bus ride home and talked to me about everything that popped into his head. Books and big words and his roommate's nicotine addiction. I was disappointed when we arrived back home because then he had to take a breath.

We walked to the bike rack where we had to part ways, and he squeezed my hand before releasing it.

"Well, Jovial," he said, a hint of regret evident in his voice. "Did you have fun?"

I nodded. "Did you?" I asked.

He smiled brightly. "Of course. I got to spend my day with you."

I bit my lip and glanced away. His intense gaze was hard to meet.

"We should do something like this, again," he proposed.

"You mean, like a date?" I stammered, embarrassed to ask.

Hesitantly, I peeked at him to see his reaction. His head tilted in question, and then he leaned back in surprise when he realized I was serious. "It doesn't have to be—"

"It can be," I said quickly, "I mean, if you want it to be."

A boyish grin graced his face and he tucked blonde hair behind his ear enthusiastically. "Really?"

"Ask me out, Bash." The confidence in my voice startled me, but I held his gaze like a blush wasn't slowly blooming across my cheeks.

"Okay," he said softly. Then, he cleared his throat and took both of my hands in his. "Jovie Underwood, I would like to formally invite you to go on a date with me because I think you're stunning and radiant, and completely mesmeric. Would you do me the honor of accepting my request?"

As he spoke, the smile on my face grew wider and the blush more fierce. The words I thought I would say got stuck in my throat, so I did the only thing I knew meant yes. I leaned forward and pressed a kiss to his sunburnt cheek.

"Call me," I whispered in his ear before pulling away.

I was completely amazed with myself, but I didn't stay long enough to see the look on his face because I was already running late. I grabbed my bike off the rack and jogged down the walkway. At the end of my block, I looked back, wanting to get one final look at him for the day. He stood in the setting sun, glowing so much that I couldn't make out his features, just shadows.

It was crazy, stupid summer love—and that was all it was ever supposed to be—or at least how it started.

Chapter 6

"So, tell me Jovial. Was yesterday a dream, or did you truly accept my proposal to take you out on a date?"

Hearing Bash's voice sent a wrench flying into the machinery of my brain. It got stuck somewhere between yesterday and this morning, causing a gate to jam and a flood of memories to unlock and drown my mind in an endless waterfall of yesterday's events. All I could feel were his fingers sliding down my arms and tangling with mine as he brought them soaring into the air while we swayed to a new rendition of an old love song. I felt the burn of the bright yellow sun on my face and heard his scratchy singing voice in my ear.

No, it couldn't have been a dream.

"I can't believe we actually did that," I marveled.

This morning when I woke, I laid still for several moments staring up at the ceiling in complete awe. Nothing felt real. How could it have been me that did all of that? I almost felt foolish, even turned to bury my face in the nearest pillow at the tingling in my gut. Then, I realized something. I didn't feel the slightest bit sorry for what I'd done. It was a strange sense of relief, but also frantic worry at the thought of the consequences. I was too far out of my norm to even begin to predict what would happen next—and really, I needed a plan or else everything would fall apart.

Bash abandoned the book cart and seated himself across from me. Again, he had managed to appear without a sound.

I blushed when his eyes met mine and then glanced down at the book in my lap as I smoothed the page.

"So, listen," he began, "if you were genuine about that date, I think you should know that I'm not a traditional dater."

A sigh of relief left my lips. I wasn't a traditional dater either—in fact, I'd never been on a date before. The thought of a lousy dinner or awkward cinema encounter made me nauseated. Those are things I spent most of my life avoiding. Besides, I had news of my own that would make those kinds of dates unnecessary.

"I don't think we should waste our time on tradition any-way," I told him. "I can only do this for the remainder of the summer. It'll be too hard after that. I'll be different."

He pressed his knuckles under his chin and studied the stress lines that formed between my eyebrows. "You'll be different?"

I sighed. "I have a friend that likes to describe me as an algorithm machine—and she's right. I take the easiest route. Distractions, setting aside time, everything that goes with dating...I'll just disappear. I have laser focus, and I'm lazy on the social front. I'm sorry."

He turned to stare out the window and pensively rub his hands together at the news. I thought I'd receive more of a reaction. If I would have said this to Quinn or anybody else, they would have immediately burst into hysterics about how selfish and unfair I was being. I was so used to everyone backing out that receiving such a calm response only made my heart beat faster in anticipation.

"That is so much kinder than just dropping off the face of the earth," he muttered with a small smile. "If other girls had given me a deadline, I would have done so many things differently."

I snapped the book in my lap shut, gaining his attention. His eyes flicked in my direction, waiting for my response.

"I don't understand you," I told him squarely.

He leaned back in his chair and stretched his arms up over his head before scooping his blonde hair into a rubber band. I watched him with a waiting expression, but he just smiled.

"Jovial," he said. "Remember. I want to feel everything. It's part of the human experience. So, don't worry about me."

Sometimes I felt like he was made especially for me. Like soul mates really existed, or that we were meant to meet. You know, fate, destiny, or some other cliché.

I had never loved before, and nobody was ever willing to give me a taste all the while knowing it could never end the way we wanted it to. Somehow I think he knew I was waiting for someone like him to stumble in and go through with this, to reveal a different part of me I didn't know existed. It was charmed, really, and he never explained why it was me he wanted to break his heart.

He said he wanted to feel everything, and I desperately wished I could comprehend just what he meant, because while he wanted to feel everything, I hoped to feel nothing at all.

I would soon find out what an irrepressible force I'd reckoned with. It would swallow me whole and leave me to battle the fears that followed me there.

"Are you absolutely positive you want to try this with me?" I asked. I'd never been so concerned about someone before. Feelings were easily dismissed, but not with him.

"Indubitably."

Then, he stood and left. But, before he got too far, he rolled the book cart back toward me and dropped a book in my lap. But it wasn't a normal book, it had spiral binding and a bookmark stuck halfway through it. When I opened the cover, his slanted, angular handwriting made rows across the page in word after word after word. In the center of the page was a dull blue sticky note.

Highlight your favorites –Bash

My legs dangled off the edge of my dad's apartment landing, stuck between the wide rungs with my arms threaded through too, holding up Bash's book of pretentious words. It was cooler out here than in Henry's apartment since he started using fans and open windows over the AC. Still, the baby hairs that poked out of my ponytail stuck to the back of my neck and my whole body shone with sweat.

obsolete

clairvoyant

idiosyncratic

A highlighter was stuck between my teeth, ready to mark my favorites as Bash suggested I should. It's funny, the strange things you do for the people you admire. If anyone else had told me to go through a three subject notebook like this, I would have tossed it aside and paid it less than half a mind.

This drive I had to make Bash happy baffled me, but I didn't have time to analyze it. I just did what I felt I should, because when I did a warm sensation, that wasn't quite adrenaline, weighed me down into a state of bliss.

I guess, what I'm getting at is—falling in love is a little like daydreaming. It's a hazy stroll into Neverland, a dizzying rush of unexplainable feelings. It's a silly smile permanently etched into your face and hot chocolate running down your throat in the blistering cold. I felt as though I was walking on a cloud, only half-aware of what I was doing, eyes heavy, mind constantly going back to Bash.

A small sigh left my lips before I bit down, stomach fluttering when I stumbled upon mesmeric.

That was definitely my favorite.

I leaned my forehead against one of the rungs and glanced into the parking lot. I bolted back up when I realized what prompted me to look was movement. A person, Quinn, was weaving past cars toward the building.

I unhooked my legs from their spaces between the rungs and stood to lean over the banister.

"Quinn?" Her name felt forced but sounded surprised. I was still embarrassed about our last gathering and gulped nervously when she ducked backward to glance at me, shielding her eyes from the sun with her hand.

"Oh, good. Jovie, you're here," she responded. "Don't move. I'm coming up."

I set Bash's notebook aside and smoothed my hair as she jogged up the stairs to Henry's floor. My arms crossed, hands absently brushing my upper arm as I waited. I didn't know what to say to her. We rarely quarreled, and I didn't have any intention to see her this soon.

When she appeared at the landing she was flush and scooped her blonde hair into a ponytail before making her way over.

"I stopped at your mom's and she sent me here instead," she explained when we were at arm's length. I nodded and her face pinched. "I don't like—whatever this is—"she motioned with her hands. "I'm sorry I said what I did. It's not what I meant."

"You meant it," I said, then turned my eyes down and licked my lips. "You were right, though. It's complicated."

She sighed and bounced on the balls of her feet. "You know it doesn't have to be," she told me quickly. That's the thing about Quinn. She couldn't keep things to herself. She had to say things now. "You never want to talk about yourself—like, really talk about yourself. I know I do that a lot—talk about myself. You know it's okay with us. To talk."

I smiled a little sheepishly because I was going to say something that would be hard for her to hear. If we were going to open up like this right now, talk seriously, then I needed to get this out. We were different. She kept her doors open and I barricaded mine closed.

"Sometimes you let things slip to other people, Quinn," I told her carefully. "I know you don't mean to, but you do. Everyone knows me as the mayor's daughter. They have their assumptions--but, that's all they get. I want to keep the rest just for me. It's personal."

She crossed her arms to and nodded, then she turned her face away to stare out at the parking lot. "I know a lot more than I let on, Jovie."

That made my heart beat hard in my chest. "What do you mean?" I asked.

"Whoever it is, that you've been running off to see," she begins. "I think they're really good for you. You always come back with a smile on your face." A soft smile graced hers fondly and she turned back to me. "I've never seen my best friend smile like that."

My heart continued to beat loudly in my ears and a blush slowly crawled up my neck toward my cheeks. I rocked for a moment and then let out a breath.

"I just really want him to myself," I told her, and her eyes twinkled at the word 'him', but she inhaled a little as to keep the excitement from bursting out of her. "Maybe one day I'll tell you about him."

Quinn only got dimples when she was excited, and they poked deep into her cheeks now. Relief filled me from top to toe. Somehow, I got a really good feeling from this. Resolution and closure, I realized, were some of life's greatest feelings. I wondered why we hadn't done this sooner.

Quinn bounced over, closing the space between us with an off-kilter hug.

"You are my very best friend no matter what," she muttered into my ear. "Come over soon, I need help making a celebratory summer playlist and you're surprisingly awesome at that."

She pulled away with a satisfied grin and waved as she jogged back down the stairs and dashed across the parking lot. My eyes followed her until she rounded the block and got lost somewhere in the orange sunset and the shadows it made off the buildings.

I knelt down at gathered Bash's notebook and my highlighter and decided to head in. Henry sat at the breakfast bar, face following a rotating fan as it swept from one side to the other. Oddly shaped paperweights held down his work documents.

"Welcome back, Jo-Jo," he greeted me distractedly. I fanned myself with my hand. Despite the fans and open windows, it was still stuffy oddly humid. "Congrats on mending things with Quinn."

I paused and turned. "You heard that?"

He nodded and turned his face away from the fan to look at me, but only for a moment because it was too hot. "I'm proud of you."

I cleared my throat a little anxiously and clutched Bash's notebook to my chest protectively. "Proud?"

"Yeah," he said, his voice light like his lips were wearing a smile. "It's nice to know there's a little bit of Henry Underwood in that genetic code of yours. Meredith was all I saw for a long time."

My brows furrowed some, and at first I thought I would dwell on it, but then I decided to let it go like a ribbon in the wind.

Summer, I thought.

Identity.

Desire.

Chapter 7

Bash was my haven. Somehow, he took me by the hand and set us flying into the clouds to a safe place. I loved to hear him talk in that strange slurred voice, but he had a way of making me talk too. He would stare at me with those sincere, inquiring eyes and have me undone before I even knew what happened. It was the most terrifying thrill to give him a piece of myself.

On our first real date he brought me to his apartment. We met at the library after his shift and biked to a tight-knit residential area I tended to stay away from. He lived in a large brick building that used to be single family home. A staircase that led up to the second floor had been added on to the outside of the building making it possible to rent either upstairs or downstairs. Bash was on the first floor.

He delicately threaded his fingers with mine and led me up the faded brick steps to a door that needed a fresh coat of paint. After digging in his pocket for the key and unlocking the door, he pulled me inside and gave me the grand tour.

The apartment had been redesigned for rental in a boxy way. Really, it was just one giant square with an L-shaped train of smaller squares lining the right side and back of the home. But, that doesn't matter. What matters is that it was nearly one-hundred percent Bash. Nobody could convince me he had a roommate sharing the space.

Overflowing bookshelves lined open walls with leaning, sometimes toppling towers of books stacked on the floor beside them. Sticky note reminders were on the back of the front door so that Bash wouldn't forget anything when he left in the morning. Unread newspapers and half-eaten takeout boxes cluttered the coffee table. Sunshine fell through large un-curtained windows to illuminate every piece of dust. He lived in his own personal library.

"Home sweet home," he announced proudly and led me to the second door of the L-shaped train of rooms. "My room," he told me.

I poked my head in. It was the same deal. A desk in the corner was all muddled with notebooks and pens and small cactus I presumed was the only plant in the whole house. His walls were blank and floor mostly bare beside a couple stray books. It was his bed that struck me as odd. There was no box spring. It was just a mattress on the floor.

"Interesting," I commented, nodding at it.

He shrugged, but tightened his hold on my fingers. "No place for monsters to hide," he told me coolly with a wink.

"You are...bizarre."

He laughed and then seemed to remember something.

"You highlighted idiosyncratic," he stated of my choices in his notebook of pretentious words. "Perhaps that word is better suited to describe my quirks."

"I liked the way it sounded," I admitted a little embarrassedly, "But I don't know exactly what it means."

His eyes turned up toward the ceiling in a thoughtful manner, like he was searching the archives of his brain for a definition.

When he found the right words he explained, "Just that I have habits or characteristics that someone identifies as individual to me. They're my quirks."

With that, he untangled our fingers and slipped past me to kneel down and sprawl out on his bed, sinking into the mattress as he stretched and relaxed. He even kicked his shoes off. "Join me?"

I nervously glanced over my shoulder and cleared my throat, contemplating his offer. I admit, it was weird, but after taking a prolonged breath I slid out of my flip-flops and joined him, leaving a considerable amount of distance between us. I laid down on my back and stared up at the blank white ceiling wondering why on earth we would just lie in bed. I underestimated what he meant by not being a traditional dater.

For a while I just listened to the sound of him breathing and inhaled the scent of his bedding which smelled exactly like how he smelled when he wasn't in the library: amber and detergent. I wanted to wrap myself up in it.

"You use so many words I've never heard of," I told him in the buzzing silence.

"Do I?" He asked breathily, like he'd been pulled back from dozing off.

"Yes."

A moment passed between us.

"Well, good," he finally replied in a cheery tone.

I tilted my head so that I caught a glimpse of the side of his face. "Good?" I wondered.

"Well, I'd hate to bore you with plain, overused English," he told me with exaggerated facial expressions. "That's how people lose interest. They hear the same old things until they're tricked into believing that's all there is."

I exhaled lazily and then swallowed a sudden rush of nervous butterflies back down. "I guess I won't be losing interest, then," I muttered mostly to myself, but Bash caught it too.

He jerked his face in my direction and held my gaze. He could be so intense. Shivers tap danced down my spine and left my cheeks rosy. Experiencing all of this for the first time was overwhelming, and I absently wondered how people could let themselves fall into infatuation every day. I wouldn't be able to do it. I felt vulnerable. This longing was desperate, maybe long overdue.

"What was it like, L.A.?" I asked suddenly, to steer myself off a dangerous path. It was a strange feeling, this time with him. A restless feeling in my bones was driving me to fill extended moments of silence with chatter. What was I expecting from this date?

He released a puff of breath and turned his gaze back to the ceiling. "Loud, fast. Everyone moves at a thousand miles an hour. The people they pass are blank faces. Everything is just a blur." When he finished talking, he shrugged as an afterthought.

"I thought I might like that—a big city," I shared softly. I hadn't planned on telling anyone that, but I couldn't leave my inquiries empty if I brought it up—even if I brought it up out of nervousness. "Nobody knows or cares who you are, what you were. They're so focused on the present, on moving forward and I want to get where I'm going as fast as I can."

"And why is that, Jovial?" he asked, raising himself onto his elbow, giving him a little height over me. "Why are you so eager to get out of Ashwood Creek and never look back?"

I let my eyes fall closed, feeling pressure in my chest. This is why I didn't like talking about it.

"None of this matters. I'm not getting anywhere here," I stated curtly.

My eyes were still closed, but I felt the bed sink as he leaned in closer to me. His fingers reached out to play with the baby hairs near my ear. My stomach twisted when obvious goosebumps popped up along my arms. "Is that why you're so distant with everyone, why everyone is given a deadline?" He asked softly.

I bit my lip, hating that he could coax me into saying things like that—things I held back for so long, that I didn't want to explain to people. Truthfully, I wanted to be a like a storm cloud. I wanted to let loose a torrential downpour of my most troublesome worries. But, if I did, I was afraid I would soak him. My fears would weigh him down until he had to crumple to the pavement, shielding himself from the relentless pound of my heavy rain. I was afraid he'd run for shelter instead of brave the shower.

"I want to be your haven," he murmured reassuringly. "I want you to trust me—even if this ends after summer."

My eyes fluttered open, and I rolled onto my side so that I faced him squarely. It was going to rain after years of drought.

"I don't want to care too much," I began, keeping my eyes steady on his shining blue ones. "I don't want people feelin g...obligated to do things for me or vice versa. I just want to do what I do and move on. There are things that don't end up mattering in life, and I don't want to get caught up in it. That's why I'm distant."

His finger trailed down the side of my face, falling to the mattress beside my arm. "Do you figure, then, that I won't end up mattering?" I could tell he was trying not to sound wounded, but he'd sewn his heart onto his sleeve a long time ago.

I shook my head. "You'll always matter because I've broken every one of my rules for you."

The idea petrified me. I had always known that giving parts of yourself away is like burying treasure. Eventually, you're going to have to go back to them, whether in body or spirit, to reclaim what they have: memories, photographs, awakened yearnings, wadded up underwear. One day, you'll stumble back across it and dig up what you thought you almost for-got.

A warm smile parted his lips and he bent forward to press his forehead to mine, causing my heart to race and toes to curl. "I am sincerely honored." He announced tenderly, and then paused to chuckle. "I am also grateful that you are not offended by the venue of this date. Most girls might find this—"

"Strange, inappropriate, cheap?" I supplied teasingly.

He clutched at his heart theatrically. "Ouch, Jovial."

I laughed lightly and tucked my hands under my head. "Why are we lounging on your bed?"

He pursed his lips in thought. "I don't know. I just kind of...did it. I spend my downtime in bed reading. It was just natural, I guess."

"It's nice," I sighed, because even though it was a weird thing at first, I'd never felt more comfortable anywhere else.

For a few minutes we just laid there, taking each other in. I watched his eyes sweep across my face, and I noticed the stubble coming in on his chin and the ever-prominent angles that made his face exactly perfect. He wasn't alien-like at all, I realized. He was simply angelic.

Bash had fallen back on his shoulder some time ago, but rose onto his forearm again. He pressed his lips into his bicep for a moment, eyes still steady on me, and then lifted his chin.

"I have a secret," he confessed playfully while a blush grew on his cheeks.

A fire burned in my stomach, flames licking at my insides and turning my mouth dry. The uneasiness from before returned. "Do you?" I asked so quietly it might have been considered a whisper.

Gold hair fell in his eyes when he nodded, but he didn't push it back into place. "I really want to kiss you."

The confidence I feared I may never feel again after the night of the music festival suddenly surged through me. It sent a fog to blind the part of my brain that would shy away and ignited the fire in my stomach to reach new heights of scorching heat.

I reached between us to tuck the fallen locks of hair back behind his ear. "Then what are you waiting for?"

He licked his lips and smiled laughingly, slowly inching forward until our noses brushed. I held my breath when he snaked his hand between us and nearly jolted when he lightly gripped the back of my neck, his touch like an electric shock.

"You're shaking," he murmured, his breath batting my lips.

I nudged my nose against his and bit my lip. "What are you waiting for?" I asked again.

He didn't need any further reassuring. My eyes fluttered closed as our lips met in a sweet caress, innocent enough and curious. He gently savored each short kiss, meshing our lips together and pulling apart slowly. I was wound tight with the urge to take more than I could give, and when he noticed this he gripped me tight and pressed a searing final kiss against my lips. Even then, he knew when to stop me from toppling over.

His thumb stroked my jaw softly and he looked into my eyes. In them, I saw something much deeper than summer love. I saw nights under the stars and late night phone calls. I saw tearstained cheeks and spine-crushing hugs.

I saw blushing, embarrassed laughter, bare moonlit skin, bike rides, long words, and takeout. I saw a future I hadn't planned for.

Chapter 8

T he heart is a metaphor—but, you must know this already.

The literal heart is a muscle that harbors no emotion. It plugs along, pushing blood in an endless circuit around your body. It quits only when there is blockage, only when the brain cannot continue to order it otherwise.

Somehow, I think the literal heart is better at explaining love than the one you dot your i's with.

Henry dropped me off at my mother's house at the end of the weekend just like always, but there was something about this encounter that separates it from the rest.

When we pulled up in front of my mother's house, he did not walk me to the door. It's something he always did just so he could get a glimpse of my mother, to hear her monotonous tone of voice snap at him, to smell the orange of her perfume. This time, he put his vehicle in park and left it running. His seatbelt remained fastened.

I turned to him in surprise. "Aren't you coming?"

His eyes were hard on the glass panels of the front door. A breath left his lungs heavily. "You're capable of letting yourself in, aren't you?"

I blinked once. "...Yes, but..."

I didn't understand.

"I love you and I'll see you next weekend." He smiled softly at me, but the light didn't quite reach his eyes.

When I arrived at his house that weekend, he asked the same question he always asked me when the door was safely shut between my mother and him.

"How's Meredith?"

I replied the same way every weekend. "Nothing's changed."

Nothing's changed.

Nothing had changed and nothing ever would. I hadn't noticed it at first, but when reflecting upon it in the moments before I went to my front door—when I was seated beside my father with Johnny Cash singing in the silence between us—I realized the phrase had finally struck him.

The brain had stopped demanding that the heart continue to beat for it.

The naïve yearning I had always thought foolish in my father vanished right in front of me, and when I recognized it's absence, I was angered. Angered and hurt. Empty and cold. Aching for a thread of hope I hadn't realized I put so much faith in—even if it was just for comfort, even if it acted as a simple fairytale.

I vacated his car with the ring of a slamming door following me down the walk.

My eyes were following the words across the page but not quite comprehending them when a knock on my bedroom door pulled me from my thoughts. Luis's ears perked up, but he didn't stir from my lap when the door slowly squeaked open.

"Just checking in," her voice informed me bluntly.

I glanced up at my mother. We had always been so similar, even in looks. Since the day my features became distinguishable I had been told we looked identical. I guess it was another reason to align my goals with hers. Sometimes we appeared to be the same person. However, I couldn't rationally explain the frustration I felt with her since this morning when Henry dropped me off, but it was a relentless pull and I couldn't bear to look at her.

My eyes dropped to the floor.

"Jovie?" Her voice rose.

The questions that had been pestering me since morning escaped before I could grind them back. I never pried, never once had a conversation of depth with my mother. I treated her the way I saw others treat her—as if she wasn't quite human, wasn't quite approachable. It occurred to me then that I didn't know the person I was becoming.

"Why do you punish him? Henry? Do you blame him? Are you ashamed?" My voice had an edge, and I regretted it immediately. It always sounded so foolish, the sound of words with emotion. Like you were giving too much of yourself away, like you had thrown down your shield and opened up an opportunity to face the blade. It terrified me.

Her eyebrows stitched together as examined me, head tilted in question to my sudden interest. In a flicker of fear that passed her stony expression so quickly I wouldn't have noticed if I wasn't staring just as hard, she saw my shield was down.

"Our time has passed," she said in a voice that was oddly strained.

Then, in a hurried shuffle, she left my room.

"We met at the best part of a person's life, somewhere between young and dumb and quarter life crisis," I read aloud, using the book to block my face from the sun.

"That's an absolute gorgeous way to begin a novel," Bash chirped from where he lay across my middle, staring up at the clouds with his book of pretentious words opened on his chest and pencil bouncing against his lips. "Simply splendiferous."

I lowered the book and snorted. "Is that even a real word?"

He lifted his book of pretentious words and turned the pages until he was near the end. "Splendiferous," he recited, "meaning splendid, magnificent, or fine."

I laughed. "You made that up."

"Jovie," he argued with a definite sense of pompousness he knew would make me roll my eyes. "I only fill this notebook with words I've read, so of course it cannot be made up."

"Of course," I taunt.

He pinched my side, and I lightly let the book drop on his forehead. With that he rolled off of me and scooched up toward my face.

The summer was coming to a close. Already the unbearably hot days were tapering off to be pleasant. The park outside the library where we were lying on his break was quiet of children. Only the trickle of the stream was audible when neither Bash or I made a sound.

His shadowy face looked down at me past his long hair, a sneaky smile softening the sharp angles of his cheeks. When he looked at me this way, my limbs turned numb. I had learned to guess what followed.

Slowly, he lowered his lips to mine, and warmth incomparable to the sun spread from my chest.

I wasn't ready to give this up when summer ended. It felt too abrupt, and he was so intoxicating.

Dangerous, dangerous, dangerous.

His fingertips traced my jaw and I pulled away. He looked down at me with a hazy, half-lidded gaze.

His jaw clenched. "Summer" was all he said.

I let out a deep sigh of regret.

"I wish the summer was longer," I admitted, and then squeezed my eyes shut because it sounded ridiculous out loud.

He didn't say anything for a moment. "You said you will be different."

"It's true," I tell him, and think of how my mother left my room so quickly I felt the wind of her stride. "I have a responsibility to myself."

Bash rolls onto his side and catches a loose strand of my hair in the wind and tucks it behind my ear. "I want you to know that I meant what I said about being a haven. I can stand to be on the back burner. I will be at the tail-end of your affections. I will sit back and wait for you to want me—to want to escape all of those responsibilities. I can let go, but I am selfish, Jovie, and I'm not ready yet. You're not ready either, I can tell. It's okay to have this, to want this."

I swallowed and averted my eyes. "The longer we do this—"

"Perhaps we will grow tired of each other."

I turned to him. "And if we don't?"

"Then break my heart, Jovial." He sat up. "Whenever this ends, it's up to you. A summer fling, a solid year, somewhere in between...it will all have the same effect."

The thought of my parents flashed across my mind. I sat up to face him. "That's what I'm afraid of. I don't regret this, but I'm fearful..."

"That you've felt too much?"

"That I will make a mistake. One I won't be able to face."

Bash pulls at the grass beneath us, his eyes cast toward the ground, staring past the earth. "A person's past is reflected in the decisions they make in the present and the way they interpret the future." His eyes lifted to mine, his magnetic gaze holding tight, reassuring somehow. Each new word rang in my ear, his voice clearer than before. "You may never tell me about your past, and that's okay. The mystery is part of your allure, and I never want to strip you of the quality that I found attractive in the first place. I just hope that one day you may recognize that you are not the mistakes of your past. You are the decisions you make for the future. You just need to have the courage to take the risk—to change the course if you aren't satisfied."

I kissed him, then.

I kissed him with a fierceness I didn't know I possessed. He made me feel human, not like the algorithm machine everyone assumed me to be—what I assumed myself to be. He somehow unearthed emotions I had never felt before. I tasted freedom on his tongue and confidence on his lips. His grip on me was a stronghold of liberation. The hair tangled in my fists, an anchor of reassurance.

The human journey is an evolution. He urged me to take the plunge.

By god, if I knew what I was feeling at the time, I would have said it sooner.

I loved him, but I didn't know how to articulate it, yet—and I wouldn't for a long time.

Perhaps we fell too fast; perhaps I wasn't brave enough to ride the inspiration out. If I knew how this would end, if I could have comprehended all of this sooner, I would have said something more profound than "summer isn't long enough" against his lips. I would have said "I'm in love with you." Because by the time it dawned on me that it was love, I was already too late. We were already saying goodbye, and I worry our time has passed, now.

His hands pushed my hair back. "There's not a word in the universe to describe how I feel right now."

"You could show me instead," I breathed.

And he did.

Chapter 9

Quinn had our celebratory summer playlist on loop while we sat side by side atop her bed, both with empty Word documents glaring at us. She had a stack of college letters between us, and a list of everything she would need to apply to each one stuck between her fingers. My head rested on her headboard, eyes staring blankly out at her tidy bedroom—particularly at her closet door, which was burdened with a plethora of pictures taped to its exterior. Everything I worked so hard for all my life now dangled just out of my reach by a college that may or may not accept me. I let out a deep groan.

"This is madness."

Quinn laughed a few melodic notes and sat up. "Which part? The essay or the recommendations? Perhaps the list of extra-curriculars? Your GPA? The transcripts?"

I groaned again, this time louder. "The fact that I have to be so thorough about a school."

Quinn agreed by nodding. "Well, at least you're set, Miss 4.0. Plus, I know you've got an impressive list of volunteering to brag about."

"Thanks, Mom," I quipped.

"It's harder for me, that's all," Quinn continued with a pout. "I'm a B-average at best. Thank God you dragged me along to some of your mom's projects, otherwise I'd be screwed. The only other thing worth noting is that one year as a cheerleader and the two school productions I had minor roles in. Clubs are lame."

"They are," I agreed with little enthusiasm. "Where are you all applying?"

"In-state universities, mostly." She shrugged. "What about you?"

"Everywhere. Anywhere but here."

She rolled her eyes and rocked herself into my shoulder. "Ashwood Creek isn't so bad."

"You're not the face of the biggest scandal in town," I argued, though futilely since she always had a counter for everything. Quinn thought she was going nowhere, but I always thought she'd make a fine lawyer.

"Nobody remembers that. They see you now, and you're a huge success," she told me earnestly. "Gosh, you should hear the way Meredith brags about you to my mom."

My brows furrowed. "My mother brags about me?"

Quinn nodded, smiling hugely. "Yeah, she was just over the other day all proud about you getting a letter from Yale—congrats, by the way."

"It was just a letter of consideration," I mumbled with a blush. "Well, she never said anything to me about it. Just told me to check the mail for something important and then disappeared. Pretty typical."

Quinn's eyes lowered to her lap where she took time examining her chipping nail polish. I tucked hair behind my year and settled back to gather my thoughts for an essay, but before I could type anything, Quinn spoke again.

"I know it's none of my business," she began a little hesitantly, remembering how our last argument ended. "But, I really think you guys need to sit down and have a heart to heart."

I groaned at how ridiculous that sounded. My mother and I? Have a meaningful conversation? We were not so emotional.

"Oh, come on, Jovie!" She pressed upon seeing the discomfort distort my features. You're nearly eighteen and the last time you two had a nice long hug was probably elementary school."

"It's...hard to talk to her," I explained with frustration hanging in my voice. "I kind of blew up about Henry to her the other day and she ran away. We can't talk about anything deep without getting awkward. Neither of us are open enough for that."

"Then get open," Quinn insists. "You're going to leave for college and likely never come back. I know you." She paused, waiting for me to argue, but I didn't deny her claim so she continued. "Are you really going to have a clear conscience if you leave your relationship like this? You weren't just raised by her, you were raised by Henry too. You can get emotional, I know you can. You must be emotionally invested in this guy you're seeing if you're hiding him from everyone. So, woman up."

I buried my face in my hands so that she couldn't see the look of complete and total defeat. She was right, I knew she was. I was emotionally invested in Bash. I was devastated when I saw Henry give up on my mom. I could be that way, it's just something I was ashamed of doing in front of my mother. She made me self-conscious about my feelings because she always pushed everyone away. I grew up thinking that's how it had to be. I was confused because Henry was different—and she was always so critical of him. I always thought I had to suppress everything, and I was wrong. She was wrong. The problem was, after I figured that out I didn't know how I could confront her—couldn't imagine a single possible scenario that led us down that path.

I felt Quinn's hand on my back and then her guiding me into her side. "Just go for it. Demand answers."

This made me laugh a little. "You're so confident."

"You're good at everything you do," she assured me. "You'll find a way to talk to her."

"Maybe."

The thought of confronting my mother about everything in our relationship from the distance we put between us to my insecurities made me nauseated. I was so nervous that every time I thought I bought myself a chance, I would immediately back out and lock myself in my room with Luis.

I was definitely going to have this discussion with her, I just didn't know when.

I went to Bash's apartment on the last day of summer so that he could proofread a few of my college essays—a task he insisted on doing even though the idea made me anxious. Just the thought of future and Bash in the same sentence made me want to bury my head in the sand much less the literal Bash holding my literal future in the literal palm of his hands. Holding onto Bash past his summer deadline was a huge deal in itself.

Never mind all of that, what really mattered about today was his roommate. I had never met his roommate before that day, but when I let myself in using the key from the hanging plant, I found him perched on the sill of an open window smoking in sweatpants and reading the back of one of Bash's books.

He stopped mid-drag and glanced at me with a sort of suspicion that passed within the couple of seconds he took to observe me. He had thick brows that unfurrowed when he glanced down at his feet and let out a puff of smoke with a short laugh.

"You must be Jovie," he said in a scratchy voice just loud of enough for me to hear. He held his cigarette close to his mouth as he spoke, allowing a constant stream of smoke to float near his face, and obscure his freckles.

I paused and clutched my essays close to my chest, unsure of what to do. When you spend your entire life avoiding situations like this, you sort of just freeze.

When I said nothing he continued, "Bash isn't home, yet. I'm Greg, by the way, his roommate."

Greg had a habit of becoming uncomfortably still when he finished talking. He always seemed to crawl back inside himself like the true introvert he wanted people to think he was.

I realized this quickly when, after a moment, he brought his cigarette back to his lips and lifted Bash's book back up to eyelevel, leaving me to figure out what to do with myself in a hesitant pose halfway between house and hall. The tobacco smell wafted over in my direction despite the open window, and made my head ache.

Bash was supposed to be done working at the library, and judging from what Greg said about him not being home yet made me think that he was notably later than usual.

"He should be home soon," Greg said suddenly, as though he could sense my hesitation. He didn't lower the book this time, and he flicked ash into the glass dish beside him. "Might I offer you a smoke while we wait on him? He owes me dinner—probably stopped for takeout." His detached musings caused me to raise a brow. Still, I decided to close the door and wait with him. He seemed harmless, and Bash didn't talk about him much, which I assumed meant he was boring.

I had never smoked a cigarette in my life nor did I intend to, so I declined his offer and entered the living space while breathing through my mouth to stop the smell from giving me a headache. When I leant up against the back of the couch, I noticed him peeking curiously at me from behind Bash's book.

"You're practically a baby," he joked after a moment with a crooked smile as he rolled his cigarette between his forefinger and thumb. "What're you, a little high school freshman? Didn't think Sebastian dated that young."

"Senior, actually," I replied boredly, though he did manage to catch my attention by using Bash's full name. The age game was not something I liked to play—and I didn't ask for a conversation. "And probably smarter than you," I tacked on for the sake of my own pride because he made me feel horribly inadequate under his scrutiny.

His eyebrows lifted. "Oh, I don't doubt that. Nearly everybody is."

He got quiet again after that and stuffed Bash's book back onto the shelf beside the window. Then, he turned away from me and stared out at the empty street. I watched him inhale and exhale smoke for a few minutes before speaking up again.

"What's the point?" I asked as he brought the cigarette to his lips again, the end glowing and shrinking. He shrugged and let out a slow breath, letting his hand fall away from his face and into his lap for the first time since I got there.

"There isn't one."

I shook my head. "That's dumb."

"Not every action requires meaning, ya know?" He replied and then reached into the breast pocket of his shirt for the rest of his Marlboro's. "So, want one?"

"I don't do things without purpose," I declined again, patiently.

He stuffed the box back into his pocket and then snubbed out his cigarette, dropping it carelessly out the window. I rolled my eyes, trying hard to hold my tongue. He seemed to notice.

"There's an old flower box hanging off the side of the window." He smiled at me. "I toss everything there." He stood and picked up a short piece of plywood from under his feet I hadn't noticed and placed it over the flower box. "Bash's idea. He can't stand the smoking either, and worries too much about the birds."

"Still reeks," I told him.

"Leave the window open and it stops."

"Or, stop smoking all together."

A smile stretched across his lips. "You and Bash must get on well."

Right at the moment, the front door jiggled and swept open, carrying not only a blast of fresh air, but Bash too. He didn't notice me right away since, upon seeing the takeout bag in Bash's arm, Greg jogged across the room to crowd him.

"Gluten free noodles?"

"Yes."

"No wasabi?"

"After what happened last time?"

"So...no wasabi?"

"Definitely not."

"Dumplings?"

"You honestly think I don't know you."

"Fried not steamed?"

"It's like we've never done this before."

"Oh, and Bash?"

Bash's eyes hooded, like he was waiting for Greg to say something that would annoy him.

"Your girlfriend is here."

I watched the surprise flash across Bash's face and his head jerk past Greg's silhouette to see me leaning against his living room couch. When our eyes met it was a mix of embarrassment and happiness to see me. I waved.

"Jovie, I'm so sorry for..." Bash's eyes followed Greg as he walked past me to sit down on the other side of the couch with the takeout bag. "Everything. I didn't mean to be late."

Smiling, I assured him, "It's fine, really. Greg and I were just talking about the flower box."

Bash glanced at the window and shoved his hands in his pockets a little bashfully. "Ah, yes. The Cigarette Graveyard. The part of the house I detest the most."

"Figures," Greg called out. "It's mine."

"I like you just fine," Bash told him, a crooked smile pulling at his lips. "Went through all that trouble with the take-out, didn't I? Could have brought home gluten, Wasabi, and steamed dumplings if I hated you."

Greg's head leaned back on the couch to rest just beside my hip. "Good man you picked."

I smiled toward Bash. "I know."

Bash grinned and looked down with red cheeks. "Alright," he mumbled, and then gestured toward Greg. "Hungry, Jovial?"

"We could eat." I wasn't hungry, but I knew Bash had just got off work. So, he led the way around the couch to sit with Greg, who was eagerly stuffing his face.

What started off as awkward slowly turned comical. Bash and Greg bantered over nothing, occasionally pulling me in to back one of them up. Both complained about the other's quirks. I learned that Greg was a sleepwalker and left a mess where ever he went. Still, he picked on the way Bash left stick notes everywhere and corrected his grammar.

"You should see him some nights walking around here with a pipe in his mouth—"

"It's sophisticated!" Bash argued defensively.

My eyebrows crept up my forehead at this bit of information, and I was tempted to laugh, but Bash looked genuinely mortified. It was like meeting him all over again, all flustered that I would think he was creepy for checking the registry.

Greg leaned forward to get a glimpse of me around Bash. "He writes these cute little stories while drinking liquor and not smoking a pipe," he explained.

"I don't do that all of the time," Bash said quickly.

"He does it enough."

I looked between the two—Greg with his smug smile and Bash with his closed eyes and gritted teeth.

"I didn't know you were I writer," was all I deemed appropriate enough to say in front of Greg. Honestly, I was more worried about the liquor. Finding that he had a drinking problem was like finding tarnish on a set of silver. It made my stomach churn.

Bash ignored my comment. "He makes it sound like I drink heavily…"

"The pipe is the more concerning part," Greg jumped. in. "He doesn't even light it. He just sits there with it hanging out of his mouth. It's so weird."

I glared at Greg for a moment and then turned my attention back to Bash. "How much do you drink, then?"

"I swear I take one shot," Bash told me in all seriousness. His blue eyes held mine unwaveringly. "That's it. I use it as mental lubrication to make it easier to write. Otherwise, I sit there and overthink."

That's…" I was lost for words. I certainly hadn't pegged Bash as one to use alcohol as a tool, especially since he seemed to be enormously against tobacco use. Even stranger than that was the fact that he hadn't told me he was a writer, though I could imagine he was since he spent all of his time surrounded by books. Even so, he had never been shy. But, I had my secrets, too. And I couldn't hold this against him. It wasn't astronomically disappointing. It was understandable, even. Startled as I was, I couldn't make a fuss.

"Bizarre, right?" Greg supplied.

I let out a breath. "It's different."

Bash had this worried look on his face, like he was sure this secret of his had ruined everything. I smiled softly at him and grabbed his hand, lacing my fingers through his.

"You don't drink and proofread, do you?" I teased, lifting up my college essays.

Bash chuckled lightly and tucked his chin toward his chest. "I'm completely sober for that part, I'm afraid...not that I ever get drunk."

"Well then, let's get to it." I stood up, his hand in mine, and led us to his bedroom, ready to accept his quirky little secret and live with it.

Before we could enter, however, Bash turned back toward Greg.

"You better believe I'm going to make you suffer for this," he said coolly, just a hint of a threat detectable.

Greg snapped open a beer and held it up between us, a devilish smile gracing his face. "Cheers."

After watching Bash pull apart my essays line by line and listening to his suggestions for over an hour, I called for a break and made for the door.

I hated it, hated all of it. Bash, with his slurred voice and gentle fingers caressing my thigh as he explained sentence combining to me. It made me want to end everything right then and there. I needed air.

No, it wasn't him correcting me. I was thankful for that. He was helping me with an essay that would assist in getting me into a college—a college far away from here, far away from him. The longer I sat there, the more I realized how impossible this was—and then he would press a kiss into my temple and a moment of irrational hope would set my heart into a sprint.

Even with his unusual drinking habits and story writing, which he told me he didn't want to discuss when I tried to ask him about it, sitting in the back of my mind. It didn't matter—and that's what scared me, that I still wanted him even though he had become secretive.

He was holding my college essays being absolutely perfect the way he was and I hated him for it. I loved him, and I hated it because I didn't know what that meant. Did that mean we should date, really date? That he should meet Meredith and Henry? That I tell Quinn how hopelessly gone I was for him?

What if we lasted? Until graduation? I would leave for college and where would that put us? I loathed long distance. I simply did not have the patience for it. I didn't want to be the ball to his chain, and I didn't want him being that for me, either. I couldn't let us hold each other back like two dogs tied to the same post.

It was just so overwhelming. I wanted to procrastinate. I wanted air. I wanted something sturdy to hold onto.

I did not live life unstructured—and it was killing me because I didn't want to let Bash go. It had to end sometime. It for sure had to end by graduation, that was already decided in my mind.

I pulled open the front door and stood there, inhaling the humid summer air. But, something was off. Where it was supposed to be refreshing and crisp, there was tobacco. I opened my eyes and found Greg sitting on the worn brick steps having another smoke. When he saw me, he chuckled.

"Cigarette?" He offered as he dug in his pocket.

I closed the door behind me and sunk down beside him. "Sure," I heard myself say.

"What's your reason, then?" He asked, going back to the conversation we had before Bash arrived.

"It's my last day to do whatever the hell I want. After this..."

Greg handed me a cigarette and helped me light it. "What? After this you've got to get serious, or somethin'?"

"I'm always serious," I deadpanned. I brought the cigarette to my lips and took a cautious inhale so I wouldn't cough. "Sometimes I'm just careless," I said around a stream of smoke. Despite my efforts, a short cough followed.

"What a bitch that is."

I nodded and brought the cigarette back to my mouth, my eyes staring out at nothing in particular. It was going to be a mess. All these tangled knots all done up in my brain. Something would get cut loose soon. I could feel it. Sometime in the future, maybe sooner, maybe later, the bliss I knew would be replaced—and there's nothing worse than some great unknown horridness looming in the distance.

Chapter 10

My first day back to my final year of school began and ended with my mother. She woke me that morning, her orange perfume waking me before her voice could. She ran through a checklist at the front door: backpack, notebooks, folders, pencils...She had it down better than I did. Like always, before I left she reminded me to be polite and to take advantage of my opportunities. Then, I was off to school, mind turning like the pedals of my bike.

The day went slowly, each teacher repeating the same things in my ears, my counselor reminding me of everything I would need for each college application. He seemed surprised that none of the schools I chose were in state. I just smiled and left.

I could already feel the shift in myself. It turned from tempted curiosity in human desire to focused thirst in the pursuit of knowledge. My future depended on my success here, and with all of their tools hanging in my reach, I was eager to pull them off the shelf and start building without interruption.

The mere idea of taking time out of my day for Bash felt overwhelming, so although I didn't want to, I pushed him to the very back of my priorities. Summer had fooled me into thinking our time wasn't enough, I realized that the night before when all of my fears began to consume me. Now, on my first day back into my routine—back into the person that I was, I knew I'd been stubbornly foolish. My emotions were too conflicted. I'd let it all get the best of me. I lived too wholly in the moment.

Bash would soon become frustrated with my disinterest and leave. That's what he was supposed to do, and I was counting on it. I always left the official cutting of the ties to the other person. It was less painful to put distance between us until nothing was there to feel when the other person walked away completely. Maybe I was too much of a coward to do it myself, maybe a part of me knew it wasn't necessary. I isolated myself. I was scared of disappointing them. It's the only thing I knew how to do with all of my relationships.

When I returned home at the end of day, Quinn was by my side, walking while I biked at a painfully slow pace. She radiated a certain spirit that I was jealous of. She was happily oblivious to everything I noticed. She chatted away about nothing in particular as we drew closer to our destination. Only the screeching of the chickens kept me conscious enough to pay attention to her words. I would lapse, otherwise, hide away in myself.

"You look awful," she said when we stopped in front of her house. It was the first time she had turned to look at me since we started our trek back home. "Are you feeling okay?"

I sat back and forced a smile. "I'm fine."

Her eyes narrowed like a lie detector test started blaring the moment the sentence left my mouth. "You're doing it."

"Doing what?" I asked defensively.

"That thing where you think so hard you create a crisis that isn't even there." She placed a hand on her hips. "I can see it on your face."

I swallowed hard and looked up the street where the Pea Shucker was happily singing while opening pods for no reason at all. How could any sane person let their life fall directionless? How could they joyfully go about doing things that aren't worthwhile? I gritted my teeth.

"You always get this way in the beginning of the school year. Just get settled. I'm sure whatever you're freaking out about will pass," Quinn spoke again as she hiked her backpack up. "See you tomorrow."

With that she turned away and headed inside. I sat there a moment longer, listening to the Pea Shucker and the squabbling chickens, trying to let Quinn's words sink in. She's right. I was panicky in the beginning of the school year. Always had been. It's the time of the year where I dropped everything to focus on what I deemed most important—and I never understood why nobody else got that way. While my anxiety peaked, everyone else seemed cool and collected.

When my mother came home later that day, I understood why I got panicky. She called me into the kitchen and pulled

out a recipe from the cupboard. We robotically pulled drawers open to grab bowls and utensils and began to prep our
dinner. While we worked, she began a conversation.

"Did you talk to your counselor today?"

"Mhmm."

"You need to get those applications in as soon as possible.
You don't want to miss any opportunities."

"Okay."

"You and Quinn find your classes alright?"

"Yep."

"Good."

Silence.

"Everything after high school gets harder," she told me
when I didn't bother to continue the conversation she began.
"You want to be well prepared—which shouldn't be too hard
for you. We're a family of hard workers. I expect it."

I nodded.

"The goal should always be to make a difference. You
give back to this life, Jovie. No dilly-dally. When you're good
and secure, then you can have fun." Her voice was almost
demanding, like she was sitting in one of her conferences
delivering a speech. "All of this will pay off in the end."

"Okay."

She patted my back as she passed me on her way to the
sink. "Crunch time. Make it count."

I don't know why these talks always made my insides twist.
Maybe I felt inspired, maybe I felt anxious—like I was at risk
for disappointing her if I didn't meet her standards. If I had
nothing to prove, she never seemed interested.

Make it count.

She reminded me that I was drawing on a whiteboard with permanent marker. There was little room for mistake making—because here's the thing about mistakes: they can make or break a masterpiece, and you never know which it is until you make it.

It took two weeks for the panic to diffuse. I channeled most of my anxiety into doing meticulous work in the classroom and out as I finished my college applications and sent them in. After that, I curled up in front of Henry's TV with homework and a History Channel documentation of King Tut.

Henry was sleepily draped beside me on the couch, arm resting on the back of the couch, watching me scribble down answers during the commercial break.

"How's Meredith?" He asked. It's the first time the question had popped up in the past month, and it was only fitting that it came up while he was sleepy and I was working at Meredith-pace.

The brain had stopped demanding that the heart beat for it, but the urge was still there.

I looked over at him. His tired eyes reflected the television screen, and his hair was becoming increasingly grey.

"I can never tell," I admitted. I knew exactly how she operated, but I had no idea how she felt. I could only get an inkling, and after seeing her get so uncomfortable with my outburst, I could only assume there was more there than what met the eye.

"Me either." He sighed and his hand came to massage the top of my head. "I used to catch glimpses of something different...something exciting before she got pregnant. Now, I feel like she blames me for messing up her life. She always had a plan, and I ruined it."

"It takes two people to make a baby," I said in return.

When it came to mentioning me, ever, in terms of my mother's life, I was considered the mistake or the mess. That part hurt. I knew Henry didn't mean it that way, didn't intend for me to get lumped in the messing up part, but I knew what I was. That was always my struggle, making her proud and not creating more of a mess. I knew that to do that I had to be successul in life, the kind of successful that gets you a letter from Yale. Deep inside, however, I yearned for something more.

Henry detected my bitterness and stopped massaging my head to put his hand on my shoulder instead. "Jovie, I think it's important that you know Meredith loves you. She loves you more than anything else in this world."

His statement only made the fire in my lungs grow hotter.

"All she does is give me pep talks and checklists," I gritted out. "Quinn pointed out that we haven't had a proper hug since I was, like, ten, Henry. I have to question everything I do because I'm afraid she'll reject me. How is that saying she loves me?"

"Jovie," he said back carefully. "She works her butt off to make a good example for you."

"Why are you defending her?" I asked incredulously, gripping my pen so hard my knuckles turn white. After how much she hurt him, I couldn't believe he wasn't taking this opportunity to tell me I was right.

"Because how I see something shouldn't be the way you see something," he shot back crossly. "My relationship with her will always be different than your relationship with her. I'm not going to let my opinions guide yours. She loves you, Jovie. Circumstances have changed between her and I, but that doesn't mean it has anything to do with you."

I jerked away and sat up. "It has everything to do with me. Everything. You said so yourself that she was different before she got pregnant—because of me. Maybe she wasn't meant to have kids."

He looked up at me tiredly. "Maybe she was."

"What?"

"Maybe you show her who she is and that terrifies her. Maybe she's trying to make sense of it, Jovie. I know she's not motherly, but she cares. Maybe she wants you to succeed so badly because it validates her as a parent. Maybe she doesn't believe in herself." He looked at me pleadingly, like he understood something I didn't, something she might have told him—although that didn't make sense because they so much as said hello to each other. "She didn't want to be a mom. She thought she would be bad at it, that she was too selfish to handle it. She was scared you wouldn't feel loved. Jovie, if you really don't feel that way, then you need to tell her because the last thing she wanted was for you to feel unloved."

I stared at him, my stomach churning and guilt weighing down on my heart. I was holding back frustrated tears until this point, and I could feel them spilling down my cheeks, now. "She's an adult," I choked out. "She's supposed to have it figured out. She's always preaching that I need it all figured out...why..?"

I broke down and Henry reached for me, pulling me into his arms to hold me while I cried, long and hard.

"I can't talk to her," I sobbed into his shoulder.

"You can talk to her," he muttered in my ear as he rubbed my back. "She's only as scary as you make her out to be."

My voice was muffled when I argued, "As she makes herself out to be."

"I think it's a defense mechanism," he said gently. "You two need to stop being scared of each other. Meredith has no excuse, and neither do you. She raised you to be strong. Make her proud."

I buried my head further into his chest and nodded. It was time to do as Quinn had suggested. Demand answers.

I called Bash that night, after my tears had dried all sticky on my skin and Henry left to go to sleep.

He answered in his signature low voice that made my insides feel like they had hot chocolate sliding down them. "Jovie?"

"Hi, Bash."

"How...astonishing it is to hear your voice," he teases, though there is a sadness laced with his words. "I thought you gave people deadlines instead of dropping off the face of the Earth."

"I gave you a deadline," I told him, "And I didn't stick to it—so I guess that means I plan on keeping you around for a while."

He delivered a short chuckle, and cleared his throat. "I didn't know zero communication was your way of putting me on the back burner. I admit I was aggrieved."

"I worked myself up and got overwhelmed," I confessed, wrinkling my nose at his formality. "I'm better, now. I miss you."

"I work tomorrow. Come see me," he suggested, his voice was perkier, but he seemed careful. I closed my eyes sadly, hating to hear that in the person I saw as indefinitely cheerful—as a haven, strong and sure.

"Okay," I agreed. "And, Bash, I was wondering something."

"Anything."

I bit my lip, knowing this was a bold request. But, if I was going to break the ice with my mother, I needed to conjure something from within her. Bash would help beautifully. He had a way about him that made everyone trust him, a lingering effect that made people open up.

"Meet my mother?" I asked.

"It would be my pleasure," was all he said.

Chapter 11

Announcing to my mother that Bash would be attending dinner with us the following weekend was more terrifying than getting on a bus with a complete stranger to see an out of town concert. It was ten times more nerve-wracking than a dozen college essays. It felt sort of like sleepwalking, but also like word vomit.

It was an emotional influenza.

"God, you should have seen the look on her face," I moaned in despair while I cradled my head in my hands. Bash dropped a kiss onto the top of my head and pulled out a chair from the library desks I was sitting at. "It was like she was looking at me for the first time-like she had no idea who I was."

"I don't need to come," he reminded me. One of his hands found my shoulder and squeezed. "In fact, it sounds like I might be better off keeping my distance."

I snatched at his hand and held fast. "You're coming."

He let out a breath and looked around him. Four o'clock and the sun was casting orange across the floor of the library, highlighting dust on every untouched book. Quiet page turning scraped near us as a curious onlooker made an excuse to listen in by pulling a random book off a shelf and pretending to be interested in it.

"Jovie, if you're trying to prove your loyalty-"

I shook my head. "No offense, Bash, but this isn't about you."

He glanced at his hand in mine, then back at me. Slowly, he pulled our hands to his mouth and kissed my knuckles. His eyes fluttered closed for a second, and then he looked somewhere else.

"I get it, you're stressed," he began gently. "But please don't snap at me. I don't know enough for you to become frustrated with me-and that's not for lack of trying." He rubbed his stubbly chin against my hand and met my eyes again. "I'm just trying to understand, okay?"

It was like a dart to my chest, his composed tenderness. There was an edge. One I hadn't seen before in Bash's voice. The sugary sweetness of new love disguised the tart hard candy that was hidden underneath, and my neglect had brought it forth.

The guilt stirring near the dart wound was like that damp cold you feel in your bones around late fall. "I'm sorry, Bash," I whispered. "The thing about my mom is that she's worse than I am-with the sharing and stuff...and while you're trying to figure me out, I'm trying to figure her out, and I'm lost. You're lost. We're all lost. And, I'm sorry. I didn't want to involve you. I never wanted you to meet her-and now you are because it's the only way I can think of that will make her...I don't know, feel something. Share something? It's...so complicated."

One corner of his lips turned up. "You're using me to get your mom to open up?"

I cringed at how horrible that sounded out loud. "Sort of-I mean, I genuinely like you, and this wasn't my, you know, master plan from the beginning or anything...you're just kind of convenient." My grimace only deepened, but Bash stood and leaned over to kiss the corner of my mouth.

"No relationship is a coincidence. I've been waiting for this." He steps around his chair and pushes it in. "I've got to get back to work, Jovial. Don't be a stranger."

With the book cart in the lead, he moved down the nearest aisle and disappeared. How he did it was beyond me. He fixed some things, left others undone, and held everything together with temporary bandages when he knew better than to dwell. I think maybe it was his way of creating his own perfect masterpiece fit for a storybook.

My mother avoided me most of the week. We chatted politely at dinner and that was it for the first half of the week; but it was so uncomfortably tense I ended up spending the other half at Henry's to escape. However, Friday was the day she was meeting Bash, so I had to be there.

When Meredith came home from work that Friday, the first thing she did was find me. Usually, she takes time to change out of her work clothes, but today was different.

There was a hesitant knock on my door, then without pausing, she let herself into my room. I glanced up from my homework and felt my insides constrict.

"What time is...your...Bash coming?" His name sounded a little funny coming from her, like she wasn't sure if his name was a real word-and, well, maybe it wasn't.

"In an hour," I replied slowly. "But, um, he wanted to help with dinner, so don't start cooking."

"He wants to help?" She asked, eyebrows hiked high on her head.

I nodded. "Something about chivalry-I don't know."

To my surprise, she grinned, and I felt myself relax. Then, she came to sit at the end of my bed and I closed my book.

"I know you think I'm mad," she said. My eyes widened, feeling a little like a deer in headlights, not sure which way to run. This could go one of two ways.

"Aren't you?"

She shook her head, and then sighed and placed a hand on the closest part of me, which happened to be my shin. "Jovie, your dad told me what you thought about me."

That made my heart pound and my cheeks flush a brilliant maroon.

"I guess I passed on some pretty bad traits, huh?" She looked me in the eye, and it felt like an apology. "Jovie, I want you to know that I don't regret bringing you into this world. I regret what happened between Henry and I, but I don't for a second regret you, okay? You're my favorite accident-the best thing that happened to me."

I stared at her for a moment, and she stared back, her eyes shining earnestly. So, I let out a deep breath, and then tossed my homework aside so I could scoot down my bed and embrace her. We were both a little awkward, arms not quite sure where to hold, and I held my breath, but we hugged, and tightly.

"So, I'm...not disappointing you...with Bash?" I asked quietly as I sat back. I feared I might shatter whatever this moment was if I spoke too loudly.

She squeezed my shoulder. "We'll see what I think of him first."

Bash arrived in a nice button-down and slacks with his hair tied back and a bouquet of wildflowers in his hand.

The long hair. That's what caused me to glance at my mother, who shook his hand a little stiffly. I couldn't read the expression on her face.

"Miss Sinclair," Bash greeted her respectfully as he handed her the bouquet. "It is an honor to meet you. Jovie absolutely reveres you and has made it explicitly clear how important this is to her."

This made her eyes slide in my direction, her lips turning up slightly like she might laugh. And, that was just Bash's way. His elaborate formalities made everyone look at him funny-even my mother.

"Your name is Bash, then?" She asked, bringing the flowers to her nose and sniffing tentatively. Hippie parents. That's what she was thinking. I could see it in the way she ever-so-slightly wrinkled her nose.

"Well, it's Sebastian, really. Sebastian Daley the Third," he told her. "It's a bit of a mouthful, though. Real confusing at Christmas. My grandmother screams Sebastian to get my granddad's attention and three of us look up. I've only got an identity when people call me Bash."

"Alright, Bash," she said.

There was more polite chit-chat, and then we moved to the kitchen where Bash insisted he retrieve the vase from the top shelf for my mother's flowers. After that, we struggled to find a rhythm in the kitchen while we cooked dinner.

My mother and I knew where everything was and Bash was like a chicken with his head cut off. Both my mother and I ran into him several times before we decided he stay by the stove and keep an eye on the pasta and the vegetables while we did the moving about.

He was reluctant and embarrassed about that despite my reassurances.

"Stir the vegetables," my mother would say curtly.

"Okay," he would reply with red cheeks. "I'm really better at chopping..."

"No," she would tell him, and he would send me a look of total helplessness and regret.

"I think I stepped on her feet and now she hates me," he muttered in my ear while I fiddled with the spice rack.

"You're fine," I whispered for the nth time. I looked over my shoulder at her placing rolls in a pan. Her face was concentrated as usual. "She would be glaring daggers otherwise. Besides, she actually talked to me before you came."

"Oh, really? I thought you two were avoiding each other."

"We were. And, I'm not really sure what all happened or why, but we ended up hugging. So, really, this is going better than I thought it would."

He took a turn looking back at her. "Is she usually...distant, or is it just me."

"Oh, no, this is normal," I said of the shallow conversation and systematic dinner preparation. "She's not the mom-home-makery type."

"Anything I should avoid saying?"

I shrugged. "Don't be philosophical because she'll shut you down. Also, don't ask about distant family-or family at all. She gets weird about that."

He nodded, and then we jumped apart because my mother was suddenly behind us asking if we could scooch out of the way.

When we finally sat down to eat, Bash thanked her a million times for allowing him to come to dinner, and then complimented her cooking a million more times than that.

Finally, she set her utensils down and folded her hands. "Bash," she said, and I felt his foot twitch beside mine. "I don't like brown nosers."

He cringed. "I apologize."

I watched his fingers tap impatiently beside his dinner plate, and I knew he wanted to say more of what she didn't want to hear anymore-because that's the only thing he thought he could do, compliment her until his tongue bled. It was strange to see someone who wore his feelings openly at this dinner table just by sitting there. I had learned to hide any emotion under a suit of armor, but all of his soft spots were exposed--even without being able to string together impressive analogies about life in her presence--and I don't think my mother knew quite what to do-because every time he twitched, she stopped to watch. She looked very confused in an unprofessional setting. I thought about the awkward hug we shared. Soon after that, she abruptly left my room. Now, as dinner was reaching its end, she started rushing things along.

"Thank you for this lovely evening. I'm sorry my foolishness was intolerable," Bash said at the door.

My mother sighed. "You were very polite. It was nice to meet you."

They exchanged another handshake, and then I followed Bash out the front door.

"Thank you," I told him.

"That wasn't so bad."

It really hadn't been. Besides the predisposed awkwardness of a parent-boyfriend meeting, it had been fairly pleasant. I knew my mother was uncomfortable with Bash's emotional vulnerability, which was obvious all night, but I had planned for that. She didn't ask him to leave and she didn't run off somewhere, so I considered this night to be a success.

I shared a brief kiss with Bash and then went back inside. My mother hadn't moved, though her arms were crossed and her eyes staring out at something far off in the distance.

She wrapped up the night by saying, "He reminds me of Henry," and then disappearing.

I didn't think much of it then. I just felt a sort of sadness weigh on my heart.

Now, I realize it was the cruelest thing she could have said, because if I was like her, and he was like Henry, this would go up in flames.

Chapter 12

Quinn sat beside me listening intently to Zoey's exaggerated boy drama in the school cafeteria. I tried to mirror Quinn's absorbed posture, and nodded along when prolonged silence called for it, but my mind was elsewhere.

It amazed me how open other people were. Zoey cussed over a boy she wasn't attached to. She heatedly recalled an incident where he insulted an aspect of her personality and refused to apologize. He was attractive, but he wasn't nice. It was the singular most confusing thing I saw in everyone around me: they kept going back to take a sip of poison because it tasted like candy.

When Zoey finished ranting, she got up and left with Noel at her side and I heard a heavy sigh come from Quinn.

She pursed her lips and rested her arms beside her tray. "I know what you're thinking," she guessed.

"That people don't know when to quit?" I said blankly while spooning rice onto my utensil.

She gave me a look that reminded me how much she loved being young and dumb. "Would you quit on your boy toy?"

"Yes," I replied so quickly the word was almost unrecognizable. I had to hold back shooting her a dirty look for her use of the term boy toy. She thought what I had with Bash was a fling, and I guess it was supposed to be. But, it wasn't anymore. It hadn't been for a long time. I cared about Bash.

"Really?"

I turned to her with frown. Lately she'd been trying to pry little details about Bash out of me. It drove her crazy that I didn't want to share everything with her. She said she'd wait for me to say something, but she was getting antsy. That's just how she was.

My mother knew now, though I couldn't really tell how she felt about Bash—and Henry, well Henry had picked up on something a long time ago, but he never pushed a discussion. I should be comfortable enough to talk about Bash to Quinn, now. But, I didn't want to discuss Bash like that. I liked the privacy I had with him. Besides, how was I supposed to say things to Quinn that I couldn't even stomach saying to him?

"Really," was all I said seriously. It was all I could give her and I didn't even know if it was true.

She groaned, dropping her chin to her chest. "Are you ever going to tell me about this mystery man?"

I shrugged. "I don't want to jinx anything."

"Would it jinx you to tell me his name?" she wondered pressingly, scooping blonde hair off the back of her neck like she was getting hot with impatience.

I tapped my fingers on the freckled surface of the lunch table thoughtfully. Her eyes found mine and held contact, cornering me. She probably thought I didn't trust her. I was beginning to grow worried that she was offended.

"Uhm...his name is Bash. Bash Daley," I finally breathed out.

"Bash." She tested the way his name rolled off her tongue, smiling a little at her success. "Jovie and Bash....Has a nice ring, doesn't it?"

I felt my cheeks warm and a small smile tease my lips. "I guess so."

She nodded and Zoey and Noel returned with icy expressions and black tongues. Like we hadn't skipped a moment of Zoey's story, Quinn and I reassumed position.

The first time Bash said he loved me was on one of those final semi-comfortable days of fall where summer still attempts to linger in the air while winter is determined to choke it off.

Leaves fell to the ground in an arrayment of yellows and reds. The mornings were a fog of icy breath and damp air. Yet, Bash wore his aviator sunglasses in the white light that couldn't cut through the thick mist, and rolled over crunchy leaves on his bicycle in a t-shirt, breathing in the earthy seven a.m. air.

I followed in a sweatshirt with the hood up, watching him silently weave ahead of me. We hadn't spoken since he picked me up from Henry's. I was still sleepy, and the cold was flowing through my bloodstream, but I didn't want to say anything. The quiet was comfortable and watching him was as mesmerizing as watching ocean waves lap against the shore.

"Fall is the loveliest season," he told me the day before, "I want to soak in the last of it at when it's at its most honest."

What he wanted to do was watch the world wake up; so, we began following this mindless route at six in the morning.

Bash looked over his shoulder at my half-lidded eyes with a serene smile. "Peaceful, isn't it?"

My voice was a scratchy reply, "I could fall asleep."

"Do you want to stop?"

I shook my head, but he still came to a slow stop before a closed corner shop in the middle of downtown Ashwood Creek. With a gentle chuckle, he leaned forward and dropped a kiss at the corner of my mouth.

"I'm sorry I suggested we do this so early in the morning. I know you stayed up late writing that paper," he apologized for the second time since he we left Henry's.

"You were writing last night, too," I reminded him. "We're even."

He watched me pull the sleeves of my sweatshirt over my hands and then pulled a light jacket from his backpack and wrapped it around my shoulders. "I like what I write about, though."

I smiled gratefully and stuck my arms through the sleeves, sinking contently into the warmth. "And what is it you write about?" I asked curiously for the hundredth time.

He always avoided the question like he was embarrassed. The second time I met him he blushed behind a book. Now, he turned his face away and scratched at his jaw. I was fond of his nervous laughter and the inquisitive look he would cast off into the distance. It made me wonder how I looked in moments like these.

He licked his lips and met my eyes with a foux confidence that made me smile. "I write about you, Jovial."

The smile vanished, but he held the coolness in his eyes like it wasn't painful. "Me? Why would you—"

"You are the single most extraordinary human being I have ever encountered," he cut in quickly, like he was afraid he'd lose his confidence if he didn't explain himself fast enough. "To capture your very essence is...the most difficult thing I've ever tried to do. That's why I drink when I do it. It makes it easier to access my feelings for you—because I find you terribly intoxicating."

He looked at me now like he was bleeding out in front of me, nervously begging with his eyes in wonderment of what to do. My mind went blank. Every word in the English language disappeared from my vocabulary for what felt like forever. He shuffled uncomfortably.

"How can you feel so...strongly?" I asked out loud.

"Because...Jovie, I care for you—I love you...and I know you don't want to hear that because it scares you, and I don't care if you love me. I don't care if you never say it back. When I'm around you it feels easy. I want to learn your bad habits and hear you laugh. You are absolutely going to break my heart and I dread it. It terrifies me. But, it's you. I'm so lucky to know you and to love you. If you walk away now..."

A few heartbeats of silence followed his hanging sentence, and he ran his hands through his hair and looked around the empty streets like he felt too exposed in this giant space. Like, nothing was tangible except for him and I but I was untouchable.

I swallowed thickly, suddenly feeling too hot in his jacket. It felt like I held out my hand with an expectant stare, so he ripped out his heart and placed it there. He challenged me to squeeze it dry, but I was too stunned to do anything but wonder why. It was so heavy.

"It would be a little awkward to walk away since I'm sitting on a bike wearing your jacket."

He paused and looked back at me with glassy eyes. "What?"

I let out a breath and braced my hands on the handle bars tightly. "I...don't know what I should say."

He squeezed his eyes shut. "Spare me and don't say anything at all. I've thoroughly embarrassed myself and I—"

"I'm not the person I was a few months ago," I interrupted. "I took a chance with you and I'm still learning." His large blue eys snapped open to gaze at me achingly. "Bash, I'm not going anywhere. This is just new."

He leaned backward like it was the first time he was looking at me—all unfamiliar and inquisitive. "I will never not stop learning you, will I?"

I reached between us and pulled him to me, pressing my lips to his with a certain strength I hadn't utilized before.

"The mystery is part of the allure, is it not?" I teased against his lips.

"I want to say something completely ludicrous, again," he admitted quietly.

It made my chest tighten uneasily. I wanted to hear him say it, but the words scared me—gave me too much power. So, I bit my lip and brushed a strand of gold hair out of his eyes.

"It will make me nervous," I warned.

His nose brushed against mine. "It will make me nervous, too."

I kissed him again, and he said those timid words, and I knew I was too far in to back out quietly and without the same detachment I would have before. Funny how that works: love. For the inexperienced it catches you like a gas leak in the middle of the night. Quiet and deadly.

I love you.

Chapter 13

Henry met Bash on the first snow of the year over beer and Scrabble in my father's claustrophobic apartment. I stumbled over myself trying to explain the relationship between Henry and Meredith to Bash in the library two weeks prior. He listened patiently as we walked down the aisles together, sliding books into their appropriate spots on the shelf.

"Can I ask you something?" he wondered that day as he fiddled with some misplaced books on the shelf.

I leaned against the book cart with a sigh. "I guess so."

"Why are you so ashamed of your parents?"

I dropped my gaze to the carpet and clenched my jaw. "I dunno. I was the result of a one-night stand between my mom and her secretary. My mother's pregnancy was an embarrassment-because, you know, being a female mayor was a big deal around here at the time-and it made her irresponsible somehow. I made her that way. Now, her and

Henry are so weird with each other, and I just feel so torn between their ideals. It's...complicated."

"Everything is so complicated," he whined with a grin. I swatted his shoulder playfully. "I have another question."

"Okay..."

"If you are so good at letting things go. If you are so good at picking up and leaving...Why don't you just ignore all of that superfluous familial background? Why do you live so purposefully in the past?"

If he thought he could stump me, he was wrong. I placed my hands on my hips and answered without wavering, "Because I live in a small town surrounded by people who have known me my entire life. Because I go to volunteer with my mother and Henry and people look between us like they're watching reality TV. Because every teacher I've ever had calls me out in front of class when the rest of the room is silent. Because I've never been able to disappear into the background without trying. And, that's not me being paranoid. If I seem bitter and distant to the people around me, it's because I learned from my mother how to avoid people I don't want to talk to-which is everyone in this town. That's why it's absolutely necessary that I get out of Ashwood Creek and start living without all this extra baggage, okay?"

Bash stared at me for a long time absorbing all of this. Being able to tell him all of that should have been a relief, but it only made me more anxious and aware of my situation. Maybe he would think I'm crazy, or that I was looking too much into everything-that I lived in a constant state of my own insanity. Maybe I would have to go back to conditioning myself to be content with me, myself, and I because being independent and lonely are two different things entirely-and I hadn't gotten too attached to him, right?

"I'm going to be very honest," he told me. "If somebody told me you'd reveal all of that to me a few months ago, I wouldn't have believed them."

"So?" I said.

He took my hand in his and held it against his chest where I could feel his heartbeat beating steadily under his sweater. "You trust me."

"I trust you," I confirm, and I was glad it wasn't my heart he could feel, because it was fluttering.

Now we sat across from Henry playing a competitive game of Scrabble. They got on so well, Bash and my father. It's like they shared this mutual connection over something I couldn't understand. I would make an expression or comment on something of little importance and they would share this look and chuckle. I wasn't sure whether I liked it or not.

"I'm afraid, Mr. Underwood, that you've set me up to take the lead by playing HAIL precisely where you did," Bash announced wickedly as he lifted a single letter from his line-up and placed it over the A.

"ZA? That's not a word." Henry snorted and shook his head.

"Yes, it is. It's the accepted slang for pizza," Bash replied smugly. "Don't believe me? Look it up."

"I will. Jovie, get me the dictionary."

"Oh, no." I lifted my hands and shook my head. "I'm not involved in this."

"I'll get it," Bash volunteered. "Where is it?"

"Side table there, top drawer," I said.

Bash dashed across the room, dodging Henry's odds and ends, to retrieve it. Henry chose this moment to lean across the protruding kitchen counter.

"Not that it matters, but I like him."

I let out an airy laugh. "I can tell."

"What did Meredith think?" he asked around a sip of beer that was meant to keep the topic of my mother casual.

I shrugged. "Hard to tell. I think she liked him, but..."

"But?"

"She said he reminded her of you."

Henry trained his eyes on the board game, trying hard not to purse his lips. I still wasn't sure if it was an insult or compliment. My mother was cryptic when talking about her feelings.

"That's interesting of her to say."

"Why is that? I questioned.

"She regrets being fond of him." It sounded bitter leaving his mouth, like he needed to rinse with water and repeat.

I could tell immediately that it was more of a personal criticism so I jerked sideways and called out for Bash. Once again, I was growing tired of my parents' mutual internalized resentment.

"Did you find 'za', yet?"

"Yep," Bash replied triumphantly as he strode across the room to show Henry. "Read it and weep, Underwood."

"I am disgusted," Henry groaned as he read the indicated passage and recorded Bash's points.

I listened to them banter for the rest of the game. I watched Henry knock Bash in the shoulder when the younger man rose victoriously above the both of us with a winning score of four hundred and twelve. Clanking beer bottles, matching laughter, a natural chemistry. It startled me how right Meredith was. In their own little way, the two were very similar. I guessed it was written in the stars then, the kind of people who fall for one another.

When Henry retired for the night, Bash joined me on the sofa to watch a history documentary. I closed my eyes and rememorized the sound of his slow-melting chocolate voice, the feel of his paper-cut fingers against my forearm, the warmth of his body radiating with mine. I counted the seconds it took for him to breathe in and out until we were silenced by our own sleepiness.

Late in the morning he finally whispered, "I should go."

"You should stay," I replied, pulling him closer.

He laughed softly and I adjusted my head to look up at the way the flashing colors from the television bounced off the angles of his face. He looked down at me through his eyelashes and pressed a soft kiss to my forehead.

"This was very enjoyable. I like Henry a lot."

"I'm glad," I said. "He likes you, too."

"You think?"

"I know," I assured him with a lazy smile. "So, he wouldn't mind if he woke up and you were still here with me."

"Why the sudden urge to keep me here?" he asked.

I laced my fingers through his. "Do you want me to ask you to leave?"

"No, I'm just a little confused. It's not like you. You like your space."

I reburied my face in his shoulder and replied, "I have me for the rest of my life. I only have you for a little while."

"Doesn't have to be that way," he muttered. "You could have me for the rest of your life, too."

I struggled to take a breath. "Bash..."

His voice was far away. "I know."

"Stay?"

"Kiss me?" he countered.

"Okay."

Bash went back to L.A. over Thanksgiving to see his family. It was the first time I became achingly inquisitive over his family. I knew he had two sisters. I knew he was the third Sebastian. I knew both of his grandparents were living. I knew the first names of his parents. But, that was it. He had met both Meredith and Henry and I was left in wonderment of what a family outside of Ashwood Creek looked like. What his family really looked like.

I knew very well what families inside Ashwood Creek looked like. Everyone around me was stuffy and nosy and held the cliché small-town Ask-If-They-Don't-Tell policy. I was itching to experience something new. I wanted Bash to take me with him, but that was unreasonable, so I stayed exactly where I was and experienced Thanksgiving two days in a row, one parent after the next.

Extended family never appeared to celebrate with Meredith and I. As far as I knew, my mother and my grandmother did not get along. They made each other incredibly uptight.

The urgency that my mother instilled in me was impressed upon her by her mother. It was this never ending trend-the pressure of high standards and unattainable perfection. One generation to the next.

That was the really scary part. I saw the way my mother loathed hers, and I could feel that same underlying dislike boiling under the surface for me, as well. I hated it. I wanted to be no part of it. I wanted to get away.

With Henry, it was different. Aunts, uncles, cousins-everyone you could think of gathered together at Henry's parent's house and ate and laughed and asked personal questions like it wasn't uncomfortable. It was like one giant family reunion. I felt so connected to them. I longed for something like this on the opposite end of my genetic line, but new it could never be. That half didn't know forgiveness. That half held grudges.

What was the rest of the world like? Black and white-how utterly confusing. I wanted to experience grey. And, the only person I knew who gave me a hint of grey was Bash. He wasn't from here. So, he had to be the answer, right? He was a little piece of the outside. So, how was Ashwood Creek not suffocating him?

The answer would make me leave him behind.

Chapter 14

On the day Bash was returning to Ashwood Creek from L.A. I went to his apartment to meet him. I found the extra key in the snow dusted hanging pot where a leafy plant had been that summer and let myself in.

He hadn't called, hadn't returned my calls. It scared me how concerned I became that my piece of grey had just disappeared. It was like being allowed to peak into heaven but never getting to live there. Frustrated with my own attachment, and angry that he let me believe he was in love, I locked myself in my bedroom to wallow in my foolishness for the remainder of my break. But, now that frustration had slow-burned its way to anger and I felt this nagging urge to confront him.

He wasn't there. When I stepped through the door, Greg scuttled out of the kitchen to find, to his disappointment, his roommates girlfriend standing where his roommate should be. Recognizing me, his expectant expression fell flat and he turned back into the kitchen.

"He's not here, yet," he called out to me in a deadpan voice.

Groaning, I stepped out of my snowy shoes and pulled off my coat and scarf. "When is he supposed to get back?" I yelled across the home.

"Now," Greg answered.

"Have you tried to get ahold of him?" I asked critically.

Greg sauntered out of the kitchen again with a reheated plate of Chinese food and sat down on the living room couch, nodding. "Three times. The library called...and there was a small fire here at the house..."

My eyebrows hiked up my forehead and I glanced around the room.

"Settle down, Sherlock. The Cigarette Graveyard sort of went up in flames. I took care of it-nothing got damaged. But, anyway, he hasn't been in contact. I'm a bit worried, but..." He shrugged. "His parents would have called if something happened."

My shoulders sunk and I let out a deep breath. Maybe it wasn't me. He hadn't been in contact with Greg, either. But, it didn't matter. His lack of contact was taking its toll. And, I couldn't bear it, anymore. This wasn't Bash. And, this annoying buzz in the back of my mind was making me feel more and more terrible by the second. I hated that feeling more than anything. It wasn't a feeling I was used to and it wasn't welcome.

I sat with Greg in silence for what felt like forever before a taxicab pulled up before the apartment and Bash was dragging a suitcase through the door, looking drained and miserable. Both Greg and I stood.

He seemed so very far away from where he were, and didn't notice us right away.

"Bash?" I asked so quietly one might have thought I was reaching out to a skittish baby deer. All the anger I had stormed to his house with had extinguished with a single glance at the pain he evidently carried with his suitcase.

His dull blue eyes lifted and he plastered on a smile for me. "Jovial, I wasn't expecting you. How was your Thanksgiving?"

Greg and I shared a questioning glance.

"Same as always...I missed you," I replied carefully.

His smile twitched and a small scowl replaced the comically high brows he wore only a moment before. His fingers fussed with the hem of his coat and he glanced down at his shoes a bit uncomfortably. I felt myself tense.

"I saw you called-but I had turned my phone off for most of my visit...and I apologize for my negligence. I feel awful about it, but...I had a surprise waiting for me when I got to L.A."

"It's fine," Greg and I said simultaneously. I pursed my lips in annoyance at Greg jumping in, but I kept my mouth clamped shut since he too had been ignored the entire week by the person who shared rent with him.

"Are you alright, or do you want to be left alone to settle?" Greg asked in a curious drawl.

Bash ran a hand through his messy snow-flake covered hair and looked between us.

"I think I just need a bit of time to settle, if that's alright." He said it to the both of us, but he stared only at me, like a private message that I should leave.

I cleared my throat, feeling a pang of hurt swell alongside an insulted bruise. In an attempt to disguise my own injuries, I smiled. He held more power over my emotions than I realized, and I couldn't let him see that.

"Yeah, of course. You probably need some time to recover and...uhm, just call me? Maybe? When you're up to it?" He nodded in reply.

It was an awkward exchange, so awkward in fact, that Greg left the room. And I was left alone with Bash to stick my feet back into my shoes and put my coat on. He handed me my scarf and helped tie it around my neck-planting a short kiss in my hair to walk home with, to melt away with the flurries.

I understood where Bash came from. I too shut everyone out when I was in pain. I walked away from everything to clear my mind, to balance myself out. I could see, now, in his expression, in the way he carried himself that something had happened-something that wasn't my fault that he needed to sort out. I put him on the backburner, now it was my turn.

What I didn't realize about my methods? It hurt to be on the other side.

Bash didn't call for three days. I went back to school, tried to focus on things that mattered, but my mind kept going back to him.

Had I done something wrong? He left shortly after saying he loved me, when I hadn't said it back. When he got to L.A., he didn't stay in touch. How else was I supposed to interpret this? I knew how I was, I knew I pushed people away-that I couldn't get too fond of people who were temporary. Had he figured that out? Had he realized something when he went back to L.A.? Had the dreariness of Ashwood Creek finally lifted from his mind to realize how ridiculous it was that he stayed with me-that he loved me?

It felt like walking through thick molasses. How had I gotten this deep? How had he gotten me this deep? Usually I was shallow enough to get out quickly, to wander about and get lost somewhere else. But, he had slowly pulled me in after him, and I was stuck now, desperate to get out even though it stuck to me and begged me to stay. It wanted to drown me, suffocate me, and I was fighting. Not me. Not me. This wasn't me.

I needed to pull myself together. If this is what people who felt too deeply felt every day, I couldn't afford staying. Algorithm machine. Find the simplest solution. Follow through. If he was releasing me-I was pulling away too.

I gritted my teeth, and pushed on.

Angry.

I didn't understand. I didn't want to understand. I just wanted out. So, I went to the library to release him.

Through the giant weighted doors, past the librarians who had gotten to know me so well they greeted me with my name-smiled brightly, offered a book. I ignored the bubbler and started up the stairs. The building was so dark now due to the snow buildup on the skylight. Every speck of dust seemed to disappear; bright yellow paint turned a moldy color. I didn't waste time losing myself among the books, I simply sat down in my usual spot in the leather chair by the window overlooking the park and waited.

As usual, he silently rolled to a stop beside me and sat down. His tired eyes and mismatched buttoning on his shirt pulled at my sympathies, but I knew I couldn't let that get to me. The nervous flutters were building up inside me, my ears were burning, and I scooted forward in my seat, prepared to leave in a rush.

"Hi," he said in his low slurred voice that now sounded weighted in an unusual way. His eyes stayed trained on the snow covered bridge outside, the same bridge he asked to meet me at for the first time months ago. My fists clutched the armrests tighter.

"I just came to say," I began in a sharp voice that rang loudly in my ears-sounding familiar in some way I refused to recognize, but he cut me off before I could continue.

"What's going on right now has nothing to do with you," he told me in a pained way, as if he knew exactly where this conversation was leading. "Like I said earlier, there was...some bad news waiting for me back in L.A., and I got there just in time to see everything...end. I've been in a state of existential trepidation, and I just needed to sort myself out alone. I thought you would understand because you've left me for ages at a time to work out your problems, but..."

I shook my head vigorously out of nervousness. "It's so out of character for you to disappear-and I didn't return your...sentiment before you left..."

"No, and I said it was okay, Jovie. I know this is one-sided in nearly every way-"

"This is not one-sided," I argued in a voice that rose above the hum of the library whisper. "This is..." I struggled to find words to explain how I felt-how it killed me to know he thought that, how selfish it made me seem, and maybe it was. I was everything I feared, how could prove otherwise if I couldn't explain my own complexity? I bit my lip and covered my face in my hands.

A torturous silence settled between us that said volumes more than our words ever could. Unanswered questions drifted between us, misunderstandings got tangled, my own fear of falling so evident alongside his ambiguous pain. Where had all of this come from? So suddenly we were off course. He had put up with me too long.

"I'm off in an hour," he announced when I glanced at him through my fingers. "Come home with me. We need to figure this out. I'll tell you my pains if you tell me yours-that's how relationships are supposed to work. I can't keep wallowing in my own mess, and I need to know that this is real, Jovie. You don't need to love me, but I need something tangible. I love you, truly. I feel everything, and it's exhilarating and exhausting and terrifying. Am I alone?"

My hands fell away from my face and I slowly shook my head without thinking first. No, he wasn't alone. I felt a hundred new things I had never felt before. And he was right, it was exhilarating and exhausting and terrifying and I had no idea what I was doing. It made me want to run, but his slow-melting chocolate voice could convince anyone to stay, to brave this uncharted territory together.

"Come back in an hour, then," I said, shaking a little. Emotionally, I was everywhere, and none of this was logical. Every

step I would have taken, he erased before me. Now, I followed his path.

He nodded, his sunray hair bouncing before his eyes. He
leaned forward in his seat and pulled a book from the cart
to hand to me.

"Letters by Lamplight," I read. "What's this one about?"

"It's a biography. I picked it up at the end of the shelf down
there," he told me, pointing to the row beside us. "I haven't
read it, so let me know if it's worth reading."

"Everything is worth reading, to you," I replied, cracking a
slight smile.

He wound a finger through one of my short locks and
smiled softly. "I'll be back in an hour."

We walked back to his apartment hand in hand, saying
nothing. He seemed to disappear in the flurries and white
light. And, when he did say something, the breeze carried it
away from my frost-burned ears. I was happy to finally reach
his apartment.

We stepped out of our wet clothing and took in the silence
of a Greg-free apartment. Then, he was leading me to his
bedroom and pulling stacks of notebooks from the piles on
his desk.

"My grandfather died while I was in L.A.," he said numbly
as we sat down on his bed. "But, not before contracting
Alzheimer's. It wasn't too bad the last time I was there. He
could recognize me, but didn't really know where he was.
Sometimes he thought he was back in the eighties, you
know? But, uh, this time he was...wild. Terrified. He didn't
know who we were. He kept asking for my grandmother,

but didn't recognize her. His liver was failing...and, I just watched him completely vanish. We were all a wreck. And I thought, what if this happens to me? What if everything I've ever known fails me? What if my memory fails and I can't remember what I've done, who I am, where I've been? What if everything I worked so hard to experience leaves me?"

I swallowed thickly, feeling guilty for believing Bash's distance was due to me. I ran a hand through my hair and shook my head. "Bash, I'm so sorry. I had no idea..."

"I didn't tell you. Of course you didn't know." He sighed. "It was a personal issue. My grandfather and I were close-he's the one who told me writing and reading was the best use of my time. He said it was the best way to leave my legacy behind: journals, stories, poetry. Anne Frank, Sylvia Plath...Give the world something to think about-that's your contribution, that's what we're all here to do, that changes the world. But, who was he? Who was I? Who is going to go through my journals, my short stories, my poetry, and odd musings when I'm gone? Somebody is going to toss all of this out." He pointed to his notebooks. "I was the only one who offered to take his journals. Everyone else was ready to get rid of them. Who cares, Jovie?"

I stared blankly at him, at the distress written across his face. He groaned and fell back against the sheets. "In the end, does any of this matter?"

I looked down at his stack of notebooks and pulled the first one off the pile. It was a black composition book with the title Sebastian Daley III #12 written on the cover. I flipped it open.

The writing was illegible for the most part, messy cursive and question marks scattered down the page.

"If I were to wake up with amnesia, this is how I would relearn myself. Every book review, every heartbreak, every mid-life crisis, every urge to escape a place where I'm too small to be heard..."

"Bash...you're anything but small. You free fall through life. You take whatever comes at you yet you chose to live here in Ashwood Creek where nothing ever happens."

"You happened, Jovie," he argued. "Nobody breaks my heart more than you, nobody challenges me more than you, and nobody makes me crazier than you. I know, because you take up three of those notebooks. If I got amnesia and tried to relearn myself, you are the person I would crave the most-and I wouldn't be able to remember the feeling of our first kiss or the sound of your laugh, and that is the worst thing I can imagine. Jovie, when this is over I don't know if I'm going to be able to let you go. That heartbreak is going to fill three more notebooks. It's pathetic."

I tossed the notebook aside and sunk down onto the mattress beside him. He was a mess, truly-an emotional being that experienced things on a far more intense level than I could imagine. And, here I was, unable to communicate everything he was unafraid to reveal. I was the pathetic one.

"How do you do that?" I asked.

"Hm?" he wondered.

"Know yourself so well, say exactly what you feel...how do you do that?"

He took my hand and played with my fingers for a while, examining the creases that compose my fingerprints and softly kissed my knuckles. When he finally caught my gaze, he sighed.

"Jovie, I'm not any better at this than you are."

"You are," I insisted. "Don't try to make me feel better."

He turned his gaze to the ceiling and shook his head. "You have to accept the good and bad things about yourself, alright? Stop being obsequious to what you think you have to be and let yourself be who you are."

My eyes fell shut and pressure built in my chest. We were both a little misty before, but I reluctantly let a tear slide down my cheek. A tear of frustration. It was the one thing I had been trying to work out since I met him. Who was I? Meredith? Henry? Both? It could be argued back and forth. But, it wasn't truly me was it? I was someone entirely new. I used to think I had it figured out. I was wrong.

"I don't know who I am."

"Well," he said softly, "I'll love you no matter what you decide to be."

That's when I knew for certain I wanted to be his-even if only for a little while. Because we all bounce back to what is familiar when we reach a fork in the road. It doesn't mean it's the wrong decision, it might in fact be the best, but it's still painful nonetheless.

Chapter 15

June 1st, 2012

I graduate today in less than three hours, but I have a confession: I have absolutely no idea what I'm doing.

I've been accepted to three different colleges, none of which I even plan to attend. I was supposed to have it all figured out by now—but maybe that's the flaw in this whole system. There's never not a flaw.

I haven't told Mom or Dad I'm leaving—not for college, not for anything. I'm just leaving. I am deserting L.A. and the suffocating pillow of whatever major I don't want.

How can I possibly go to school for something when I have no passions? Or is that what we've come to as a society? Passionless, hopeless, robots fit for uniforms of the highest paying salary? That's why I have to leave.

I can't breathe here in L.A. Everything is moving too fast. I see hundreds of people pass me on the streets but their faces are blurs. Their identities are nothingness. I cannot tell who is alive and who is barely holding on.

I'm barely holding on.

I'm getting lost in the crowd.

I can't stomach the idea of continuing this way. I'm not heard here. I'm not even seen. I'm writing pointless journals, trying to lose myself in someone else's story, and forgetting who I am. Do I know? Did I ever know?

I need some time to surface, to rediscover everything I didn't know about myself. I'll get out of town, find a quiet nook in the middle of nowhere, work a job I can barely survive on, walk everywhere, say what I feel, and just live for once in my life.

I'm tired of being nothing. I want to be something somewhere. I want to be something to someone.

Perhaps I'm unrealistic.

Perhaps this world really is about Pomp and Circumstance—and if so, how utterly awful. Be what they want or be a failure to all. Well, I refuse to stand by and witness what they have to say about me. I won't fall victim to conformity.

I'm going to be happy one day.

First step: graduation. T-minus two and a half hours.

Isn't it completely absurd how we don't believe our life begins until then? A flower only blooms when under stress.

Signed,

Bash Daley

Luis jumped out of my lap with the sound of a knock at my bedroom door. I slapped Bash's journal shut and pushed it under my pillow.

"Come in."

Since Bash got home a few weeks earlier, I hadn't been reading much else but his old journals. Maybe it was a silly sentiment that I'd decided to borrow them, but I really do think my curiosity and overall fondness made me hungry for them. Bash didn't really like it—insisted that they were for other's eyes after he was gone. But, with a timid reminder, I brought back the timeless argument that we would eventually go our separate ways and he conceded. But, since he had insisted that they were for nobody else's eyes, I made a point of hiding them. Especially when an entry made my heart race.

My mother came in with the open door and held out a letter. "I think it's an acceptance letter."

I kicked off my sheets and flattened my bedhead as I sat up, eagerly reaching for her. "Where's it from?" My voice bordered on excited and nervous, and I watched the gentle smile find my mother's lips.

"San Francisco State?" She flipped the envelope back at herself to make sure. "I didn't know you applied there." I snatched the letter from her, leaving her slightly startled and blinking in confusion. "Jovie."

"Big city," I mumbled, eyes fixed on the seal of the letter and fingers anxiously ripping at the paper.

The truth was I'd only applied to schools located in big cities or busy areas. She had tried to get me to apply to places closer to home, even threatened she wouldn't help pay tuition if I left the state, but I didn't bother listening. I knew what I wanted. I'd been under her authority for long enough. If she wouldn't help me pay, I'd apply for scholarships. It was as easy as that.

My mother sighed and cautiously balanced herself on the corner of my bed, waiting to see if I'd been accepted or rejected. Her tightly folded hands were something I noticed just as I pulled the letter out. I paused.

"What?" I asked. When she dropped off mail, she usually didn't bother staying to see the outcome.

She pursed her lips and shook her head. "If you get in, will you go?"

I had applied to so many schools I couldn't remember the exact count. Did I know for sure which one I wanted most? No. I would narrow it down by prestige and location when I'd gotten every answer back. I didn't know why she cared. She was so eager to lecture me on the importance of this step in my life; I didn't understand why my exact destination made any difference as long as I was doing as I was told.

"Maybe, maybe not," I replied. "It's already got its appeal being far away from here."

Her eyes narrow and I glanced down quickly in submission, knowing I made a mistake with the last bit.

"Do you hate me?"

I looked up, catching the seriousness in her tone with the harshness in her stare. She was never upfront about com-munication with me on this level. The straightforwardness seemed brash but stubborn to adhere. It felt like she'd been waiting a long time to come out with this, and having found the opportunity, was determined to nail the argument to its sticking place.

I found myself stunned to silence.

"Well?" she asked a bit shakily, but with a confidence not found in a city hall meeting room. "Do you think I hate you? Because I told you, you're my favorite mistake. I love you more than I ever thought possible. And, I get this feeling, with you wanting to get as far away from here as you can, that you can't stand me. That you hate me. It's eating at me, Jovie. I have to know. Is it true, or no? Where did I mess up?"

When you're up against a wall with something of a gun pointed at your head, you forget how to breathe, how to think, how to do anything but stare down the barrel and pray for an easy way out. I felt a little sick, not accustomed, and really, not very fond of the situation she was throwing on me. She had never prepared me for any sort of confrontation like this in my life. We were not confrontation people, my mother and I. It's something I knew for a fact that I'd learned from her: how to run.

"I—I don't hate you." It was barely a whisper.

She threw her hands up in a way that required too much emotional confliction for my mother to possess. "Then why do you insist on abandoning everyone who loves you?"

My eyes stung. She had never yelled at me this way before. It was like my single comment about leaving had unstoppered years' worth of bottled up insecurities and hurt. It was flowing freely now, and it wouldn't stop until it was emptied. My heart beat so fast I thought it would give out.

How had everything suddenly gotten this way? Had I missed my cue?

"Mom..."

"Jovie," the hurt rang as clear as a bell. "I just need to know what I did wrong, because my mother never asked me. I spent most of my life thinking it was my fault, and it wasn't. And, it's not your fault, either." Her eyes began to water. "We're just really bad at this."

"You should have said something before," I said softly, but firmly, not even looking at her now. "You should have said something when you realized it the first time—because this is me. This is what I've learned from you. I always thought I needed to be alone."

"You can stay here, you can stay with the people who love you. You don't need to travel hundreds of miles away to be alone when it's not necessary," she urged. "All I've ever wanted is for you to be okay. For you to be strong and ready for anything—to have a plan."

"Well," I said, lifting the letter, "I do have a plan—and I won't be alone. I can't live in Ashwood Creek, anymore. I can't be around any of this anymore. I need to live anonymously for a little while, recreate what I never got to decide for myself. All of your problems have been mine for as long as I can remember. Mom, I'm done." I shrugged helplessly. "I need to be anonymous. Identity isn't a luxury, it's a necessity. I don't have one here."

She leaned forward, pushing her fingers into her dark hairline and squeezing her eyes shut. I swallowed thickly, regretting every last thing I'd said in these past minutes. Funny how feelings work. You want to vocalize them so badly, but the moment you do you regret it. It's a subliminal message from our brain saying we've opened up vulnerability for attack. It's the panic setting in. All you can do is breathe.

"I don't understand," she finally spoke. "You preach about identity to me, but you haven't been yourself since that boy."

"What is myself, Mom?" I asked frustratedly. "That's the point."

She let out a condescending sigh. "So you're going to continue going down this path—dragging that poor boy with you until you can get away from all of us? At least I had enough sense to let your father go."

"You never let him go!" I argued. "I tie you together every day. My mannerisms, the faces I make, my hopefulness for something good in this world—that's Henry, Mom. You drop me off every weekend. Every once in a while you walk me to his door. You see him every day at work. You still confide in him, I know you do. He's the only person besides me that you trust, and you pretend you hate him, you pretend you don't care! You're the one dragging a boy around—"

"Enough, Jovie."

"You act like you have it all figured out, like you're the victim—"

"Jovie!"

"We're exactly the same, so don't judge me! Do I hate you, Mom? Maybe a little, because you're my default setting, and I can't stand that part of me!"

She stood and I bolted. I left the letter half opened on my bed and dashed from the room and I didn't stop running. I snatched money from the change bowl next to my mother's keys, and with slipper-clad feet I burst out the front door into the chilly December air, leaving footprints in the snow as I ran down the road. The chickens next door were attempting to keep warm in their hutch, not one show-tune followed me down the street, and nothing but my own gasps for air accompanied me into town.

I couldn't believe what I had done.

I needed to get out of Ashwood Creek.

I took a bus to Winsor, the place where Bash and I watched the music festival that summer, and called Quinn from a payphone with some loose change I found in the cup holder next to my seat. The adrenaline that was still pulsing through my system was making me light headed, and the cold was turning my fingers numb. I felt wild, spinning, unaware and confused. My eyes were red from forcing back tears.

"Hello?"

"Quinn?"

"Jovie?"

"Yeah, it's me."

I heard her pull away from the receiver, "Meredith! She's here!"

"No! Quinn!" I ran a fist through my hair and pounded my head against the brick building the payphone was attached to. "I swear to God I will hang up. Don't do this right now."

"She's been worried sick about you! Where the hell are you, Jovie?" Quinn demanded, her voice was gritty, terrified, annoyed—something.

"I can't come back. You don't understand. I can't come back. I said so many stupid things. I wanted to say more. Quinn, I nearly snapped. I can't do this anymore. I'm so tired."

"You need to come home. Don't do anything stupid, Jovie—"

"Jovie?" It was my mother's voice.

I slammed the receiver down and slowly fell to a crouched position under the payphone. My forehead rolled against the brick and I closed my eyes, shaking my head.

You're being so stupid. Stop running. STOP RUNNING.

"God, I just feel so trapped," I whispered in a croak, talking to that little voice in my head. "She'll never forgive me. Everything is going to change. It can't change. I just want to go back. Erase it all. I'm so stupid."

I turned my head, looking through a thin glaze of tears at the deserted streets—so unrecognizable now that snow had fallen and there were no half-drunk, sun-kissed bodies swaying to music so loud you thought your ears would stop working. Sniffling, I stood back up and held the phone back to my ear as I inserted more coins and dialed his number.

"Hello?"

"Bash, it's me."

"Jovie?" Relief echoed in my ears, and I knew he had been told of my disappearance, but from whom, I had the slightest idea. "They're looking everywhere for you. Where are you? Do you need me to come get you? What happened? Are you okay?"

I ignored all of this. "Bash, do you remember what you wrote on your graduation day?"

He chuckled lightly on the other end and commented, "I was...out of sorts. I wanted to leave, wanted to be something..."

I cut in, "Well, I want to leave, and I want to be nothing. I can't stay in Ashwood Creek. I can't keep battling with Meredith and Henry. I'm so tired of going back and forth. I don't know who I am, and I'll never know as long as I'm anywhere near where they are. I'm barely holding on, here. I need you to take me away."

There was silence on his end; it went on for so long I thought he hung up. I pinched the bridge of my nose, ready to give up, and then finally he replied, "You will never heal, Jovie. You can't leave things like this. You can't run anymore. Nothing good ever came from someone who grew a crooked heart because they tried to accommodate pain that didn't have to be there. Look at your mom. She's...not what she wants to be. You see that. Why do you want to continue the pattern?"

I couldn't stand still. "It's just easier, Bash. It's easier, and I'm tired."

"What's easy now," he told me, "is a trick. It looks pretty on the outside, but it's only a vessel for hardship and pain—and they are wonderful at disguise. Believe me. I was everywhere before settling in Ashwood Creek. I got beat up, too. I had to fix things with my parents. I had to face them when I felt like a failure. It's not easy navigating life for the first time on your own. It's...confounding."

I closed my eyes, letting his soothing voice and inadvertent wisdom lull me to serenity.

"Bash, I don't know if I can just fix things with my mother. We've never talked to each other that way before. We've never...said things before. It was unscripted and terrifying. I lost control..."

"You have school tomorrow. You have to come back. You can stay with me and Greg tonight, but I can't let you run. You don't know what's possible and what's not. You have to try," he stated in a matter all too convincing from his mouth.

"I can stay with you tonight?"

"Yes. Where are you?"

"Winsor."

He released a breathy laugh. "Why Winsor?"

"It's the furthest place from Ashwood Creek I've ever been."

"I'm coming."

It was late-afternoon when we finally got back to Bash's apartment. He called Henry, told him I was safe—told him to tell Meredith I was okay, and to let me be for tonight. I guess there had been some arguing on both ends. I couldn't quite explain what I felt for Bash when he hopped off the bus and held my hand all the way home.

He let us sit in silence. He traced the lines on my palms and pressed kisses into my hair. I had never been more grateful for him. I still can't understand how he went through what he did for me, not just then, but the whole time we called each other ours. Maybe he saw himself in the struggling bits of me that he understood. Maybe it was the only thing he ever understood: struggle in the first part of the life you really get to live. He was so fascinated with it—he wanted to answer all the questions that were to be answered there. He loved being the hero of that story.

When it was time for bed, I wore one of his old shirts and watched him journal from his mattress on the floor. No monsters could reach out and tug at his ankles when he crawled in next to me. Moonlight illuminated the high points on his face and made eerie shadows on mine. We faced each other for a long while, not touching, just admiring. Then, he reached between us and ran his thumb along my bottom lip and brushed hair from my neck.

I closed my eyes in anticipation, waiting for his lips to find mine. And they did, again and again until I had the courage to undo the first couple buttons on the old shirt I wore and for him to yank off his own. Then, there was nothing but the sound of lips coming together and breaking apart, choppy breathing, and hands exploring exposed skin.

It was the release of a low gasp that pulled Bash off of me and reaching for his shirt.

I sat up. "What's wrong?"

"Nothing. That's it for tonight. Your parents trust me—"

"I'm not a kid, Bash. I don't want to stop—I don't need to. I'm perfectly capable of understanding the cons—"

He put a hand on my shoulder and guided me back to a lying down position. "You're vulnerable from the day. You're feeling rebellious. I'm not taking advantage of that."

"Bash—"

"I love you," he said softly. "We're not ready."

My cheeks warmed and I turned my face away, knowing he was right but feeling embarrassed for trying to pressure him, for trying to seem more mature than I'd felt that entire day.

"Sorry," I muttered.

He pressed a kiss to my lips and wrapped an arm around me. "I just want to sleep with you in the most innocent way possible," he laughed.

I wrinkled my nose at him. He did it back.

"I like you way more than I ever wanted to," I admitted.

"I love you," he repeated.

I brushed hair from his face. "Goodnight."

"Goodnight," he replied sleepily, wrapping his arm around me more firmly.

Looking back at that night, I should have said it back.

Chapter 16

I dreamed about rain. I dreamed about a cold, heavy, downpour and crashing thunder and lightning so bright it blinded me. My mind was blank but my senses on overdrive. I felt too much and all I could do was scream, but I was alone and nobody could hear me. And when I woke, my throat was hoarse and my body was numb as though I truly had exhausted every inch of me. Beside me the sheets were drawn back and absent of Bash. Finally, I could think again, but memories of the day before suffocated everything else so that I was forced to sink into the mattress with the weight of them.

Quickly, I untangled myself from the sheets and found myself too close to the ground, and my legs burned when I stood while my head spun with the sudden rush of blood. Silvery winter sunlight illuminated the room, and outside Bash's bedroom door the warm glow of the living room lamps and quiet hum of the television drew me from my nightmare.

Greg shuffled past me in a rush, barely taking time to shove his feet in his boots and throw his coat over his shoulders before disappearing into the snow laden streets of Ashwood Creek. I glanced over to where Bash was sitting on the living room couch spooning oatmeal into his mouth while reading a worn-out hardcover book, paying less than half a mind to the newscaster on the television. From the odd stillness and white light forcing itself past every half-covered window I knew it was late morning and that I had overslept. The feeling made me sick, and the embarrassment from yesterday's events were quickly catching up with me.

Bash looked over his shoulder and smiled tiredly. "Good morning, Jovial. You just happened to get incredibly lucky. We got ten whole inches of snow last night unexpectedly, and the entire town decided to shut down and clear it up. School's cancelled."

I sighed. "I wouldn't say that's lucky."

He shrugged and creased the corner of the page he was reading as a bookmark. "Your mom called. She wants you home immediately."

My stomach lurched and I squeezed my eyes shut as a shiver went down my spine. Like yesterday, I felt the incredible urge to run away, to cut off all ties with her and disappear into the world and recreate everything I knew, but I knew I couldn't. Bash wouldn't let me.

"I'll get you something to eat. You get dressed. You know you have to go back," he said carefully.

"I can't think of anything I'd like to do less than face my mother right now." I opened my eyes as he stood. "I don't know what I was thinking. It's all a mess, now. She must think badly of me...disrespectful, spoiled, unappreciative..." I raked my hands through my hair, overwhelmed with my heart racing and dizzy with guilt.

Bash climbed over the couch and took a few short strides before encompassing me in his embrace. What felt frazzled a second ago, what felt disorganized and chaotic shrunk under the catch of his arms. It was as if he'd caught the shrapnel of an exploded bomb and carefully fitted the pieces together again.

"Disappointment" was the last muttered word to escape my mouth before he smothered me with his clean amber smell and reassuring grip.

"You're embellishing the situation, and in an outlandish way that's only intensifying your own stress," he told me in his silly pompous language that seemed out of place only until you listened to the richness of his voice. "No scenario is ever as terrible as the ones our minds fabricate when our thoughts are saturated with paranoia and anxiety. In other words, nothing is ever as bad as it seems. Your mom sounded worried, not angry. So, take a deep breath. You're Jovie Underwood." He chuckled. "You're sort of like a spinning wheel-and I thought you wouldn't allow yourself to teeter and fall over."

I breathed a light laugh into his shoulder and pressed my forehead into the crook of his neck. He was much too comforting for someone I couldn't keep.

"You're too good at this," I whispered, feeling suddenly at ease with only the faintest of butterfly wings brushing my insides.

He pressed a kiss into my hair and then my forehead and let his lips ghost over my skin until I unburied my face so he could deliver a kiss as sweet as his voice to my lips. It was enough to convince me to follow him into the frosty, deserted streets of Ashwood Creek and lead me to my own mother's house.

Henry's car was parked outside my mother's house when Bash and I arrived with our pant-legs soaked from having had to stomp through ten inches of snow most of the way there. It made my heart flutter. The last time Henry came past the front door was for my sixth birthday because my mother didn't want to face my grandmother by herself. And, not surprisingly, it was the last time I saw any of them in the same room together for pleasure.

As we came to the front door, I stopped and turned to Bash, not looking him in the eye. "Thanks for walking me home-"

"You know it's no trouble at all, Jovial-"

"But, you should start heading back now, before I knock." I interrupted quickly, all the while staring at my shoes.

Bash leaned back to survey me, tilting his head in confusion. "I went to Winsor to get you, you stayed the night, I walked you home...I would think your parents might like to talk to me about all of this."

My cheeks flushed in embarrassment and I looked up. "Are you talking down to me right now?"

His eyes grew at the suggestion, and he stammered over his words while shaking his head until finally he managed, "Jovie, you can't be serious. I'm trying to be considerate toward your parents."

"Well, you make it sound an awful lot like you've had to babysit me," I grumbled irritably.

I knew I wasn't truly frustrated with him. I was nervous, and embarrassed, and I didn't want him to see anything that would happen between me and my family from that point on. I could feel the same anxious tension build up under my skin that would put me over the edge with Quinn, and if I had to apologize about it later, I would. But, I didn't need him as a witness to whatever horrible lecture was waiting for me on the other side of the door. I was tired of feeling like a child-beneath him somehow when I struggled with my parents.

His face was a mix of confusion and disappointment, and I hated the way it looked-the guilt that often made me wonder why I kept "leading him on" as my mother might say. But, there was always something, like the way he refused to give up.

He held my gaze and allowed the slightest shake of his head. "You're not allowed to take this out on me. All I've done is help, Jovie."

I let out a deep breath, and the cold air froze it, turning it to wispy vapor that he watched patiently, waiting for what I had to say next. "I know," I said, trembling from the cold. "I'm sorr-"

The door suddenly swung open, and a blast of warm air was accompanied by lipgloss framed words that gasped, "Jovie. Thank god."

And then Quinn threw herself on me, arms squeezing my shoulders while I stood in stunned stiffness. "I was so worried about you."

Then, as quickly as she'd leapt on me, she was pushing herself away and calling into the house, "Meredith, Henry, she's back!"

When she turned to face me again, her eyes found Bash, who was equally as thrown off, and frozen in place to the doormat, and her mouth dropped open. "Oh my god, finally. Bash, right?" She leaned toward him curiously, eyes sweeping over his long locks and angular features. "It's about time I get to meet you." She tossed me a quick look that meant she was still unhappy about me hiding him away. "You know how Jovie is."

Bash, hardly ever lost for words, was now, and he stared at Quinn blankly, slowly taking in her bubbliness, high ponytail, and million dollar smile. I couldn't tell if he was overwhelmed or intrigued.

"Hi," was the only word that he could form. My stomach churned in mortification. This isn't how I wanted them to meet.

But, before I could say anything, Meredith was at the door, and so was Henry. And, Quinn bounced out of the way while Henry pushed past my mother to hug me.

"What the hell were you thinking?" he muttered in my ear. His grip was so tight it hurt.

When he pulled away I caught a glimpse of my mother standing in the door way with her arms crossed and her eyes hard.

"Thank you, Bash," she said to him, although she was glaring at me. I felt my stomach drop. I no longer trembled from the cold, or felt the heat in my cheeks, or cared about the ache in my feet. All I felt was sheer dread. And it made me numb. "I appreciate what you did for her, but I think it's best you leave, now."

A bit awkwardly, he agreed. And, after pressing a chaste kiss to my temple and shaking Henry's hand, he headed down the walk with Quinn calling after him how nice it was to finally meet him.

My mother now turned to Quinn. "You can leave now too," she advised.

My friend's eyes shot between the three of us all together under one roof before it clicked, and she jumped forward. "Oh, right."

After grabbing her coat and thanking my parents for letting her wait with them, she wrapped me in another hug. "Let me know how this goes, yeah? Glad you're okay."

She stepped back, holding me at arm's length to check if I'd received the message, and then shuffled past me to leave.

I stepped inside and my mother pushed the door close behind me. The silence was so deafening, my ears began to ring. I had to remind myself to breathe.

She didn't wait. Still all standing in the entrance, my mother began by taking a step away from the door and placing both hands on her hips. "So. Care to explain yourself?"

We'd never done this before-have a big family meeting. Henry was there, and stood at a distance with his hands behind his back and his head bowed, ready to listen-maybe jump in if necessary-while my mom positioned herself across from me with an authoritative stance I'd only ever seen when she was demanding something at work.

I didn't know what to say. How could I explain? I had never done one thing in my life that wasn't a part of the manual.

"Well," she pressed, dark hair falling across her shoulders as she leaned toward me.

"I..." I paused, taking a breath that would carry me through what I needed to say, what I knew had to be said. "I'm sorry for what happened. I feel so horribly about it-I didn't think you'd want me back here. I know I shouldn't have said what I did. I shouldn't have run. I'm just overwhelmed, and scared, and confused..."

"Of course I want you back here," she nearly screamed, throwing her hands up. "What the hell kind of a person do you think I am, Jovie? I don't express my feelings well, but that doesn't mean that what you did didn't hurt me. Do you understand? I have feelings like every other human being."

"Well, then why am I terrified of you? Of failing?" I shouted back, feeling my whole body flush with heat and my feet melt into the floor.

Henry jumped up. "Jovie-"

I ignored him, but kept laser focus on my mother, watching as she seethed while I spoke. "You act so perfect all the time. Every little thing that doesn't go according to plan infuriates you-and you pick, and pick, and pick until it has no choice but to be perfect. And, when you can't make something perfect, you drop it all together! If it can't be perfected, then you must not need it that much, right? If it isn't some sterile, cookie-cutter image of what you want it to be, you run."

I didn't know what all I was referring to, maybe I was referring to Henry, maybe I was talking about her relationship with my grandmother, maybe I was talking about all the little things, but it felt like spitting up vomit as it came out. It shouldn't have been said, even if it was true, and I knew it.

"That is way out of line, Jovie!" she cut in, pointing a thin finger in my face. "That is not your place, do you hear me? I am the parent, here. You sit back and listen."

The authoritative bite in her voice and her rigid posture forced my adrenaline drunk brain into complete silence. My whole body shook with exhaustion, and the regret weighed heavily in my muscles like a dull ache. The tears welled up before I could stop them.

"I'm sorry, I'm sorry..." I repeated, crumpling over. Henry caught me before I sunk to the floor-completely ashamed.

"I don't know where you come from all suddenly high and mighty," my mother fumed. "But, you know that behavior is not tolerated in this household or in Henry's. Respect-I don't know where it's gone all of a sudden. I have done my very best in raising you. This is all I know. There's no manual on how to be a parent. This is who I am, and you, of all people, are not allowed to criticize." Her voice was choking up, and she paused to blink back tears she hated people to see. "One day you'll see," she said, swallowing hard. "One day you'll be an adult, maybe even a parent, and you'll understand. It's not the philosophical idealism that your Bash seems to think is the answer-because I know that phase as a young adult. Growing up and finding who you are isn't going to happen the second you get out of Ashwood Creek. There's not going to be this great revelation. It's just going to suck. Real life punches you in the face, and kicks you while you're down. And, if you can find a way to cope with that, and it's different from mine, then good for you. I'll be proud of you, because I know I'm not perfect," she said softly, voice cracking. "But I try. And I want you to realize that it's work. And, yes, it sucks. I don't sugar coat things."

"I'm just tired," I muttered into Henry's shoulder, feeling his warm arms squeeze me tighter. "I'm tired of feeling like a machine."

"A machine?" Henry asked, smoothing the hair from my face.

I sniffled and shook my head. "Everyone thinks I'm just some robot person that's distant, and weird, and obsessively task-oriented. Quinn told me I function like an algorithm machine. My second grade teacher told me I was programmed like my mom-and I didn't even know what that meant, but I do now. And, I'm tired of it. I'm tired of having no identity, no personality, just goals that need to be completed..." I lifted my head, hesitantly making eye contact with my mother. "I push people away...like you. If they don't benefit me, they go."

"I don't do that-"

"You do." And this time, it was Henry that said it. "You pushed me away. You still do to this day. We talk about Jovie, we talk about life, we talk about anything, but then you feel like you've shared too much, or let your guard down. So, you build your walls back up and I don't hear from you for months. You do it, Mer. She picked up on it."

My mother released an exasperated sigh, and lifted the hair off the back of her neck like she was warm. "Henry, we're not having this discussion. We're talking about Jovie, and her behavior."

"Jovie is just like you. The way she is with Bash-the way we used to be. Mer...guess who she got it from? You had a crisis, too..."

"Henry, stop!"

"You want to fix this, Mer? Stop with the goddamn emotional constipation in this house. Communicate for once in your life about something other than politics and the steps to success. It's no wonder she's tired. You two are strangers." After cradling me in his arms like he did when I was young, he finally released me from his embrace and instead put a hand on my shoulder while I stood still hunched over. "And for the record, I loved you once. You weren't always this afraid. Stop letting your bad relationship with your mom affect the one you have with Jovie." Releasing me, he stretched and then went to collect his coat from the rack. "I'm leaving, now. Jovie, I'm glad you're home safe. Don't you dare do that again or it's going to be me picking you up. Alright? Goodbye."

And, just like that, he disappeared with a slam of the front door that left the air between my mother and I thick and uncomfortable. I felt like I knew less about my parents than I had before now that new parts of the puzzle were revealed.

I'd never heard Henry speak up to my mother. Not once. And now he had said his piece and left, leaving my mother and I to stare at each other and wonder what the next move was. Suddenly it wasn't just about me, it was about both of us. And, that's exactly what Henry wanted.

My mouth was dry, and I couldn't form words. And, from the looks of it, neither could she. So, we just stared at each other, finding the similarities and the differences-examining the parts of ourselves we saw in each other, and the parts shaped by other people.

"I knew you were like me," she finally said, and swiped a tear away from the corner of her eye. "I knew you'd want to leave and never come back. You weren't very old, but I could tell. So, I told myself: don't get too attached to someone with the greatest ability to hurt you. I did it to Henry, and then I did it with you. But, that's not right. That's not the way things work. And, I'm sorry for that. I'm sorry for being a bad mom." She covered her face and began to sob like I'd never seen before. Her shoulders shook, and her hair stuck to her face, and her skin burned the color of cherries.

It was the first, most genuinely honest thing she'd ever said to me in the seventeen years she'd been my mother. I felt compelled to do so, to stride forward and wrap my arms around her and squeeze her so tight she laughed. And, this time it wasn't awkward, it didn't feel weird, it felt natural.

"I love you, Mom," I whispered in her ear. "I never hated you. I just don't know you."

She sniffled and lifted her head from my shoulder. "Jovie, there's not a whole lot to tell."

"It's a lot to me."

And, like a rain cloud, she poured. And finally, I saw the sun.

Chapter 17

The relationship I had with my mother always felt like a cloudy, grey day on the brink of a thunderstorm. You walked through it cautiously, with your umbrella halfway open, praying it'd just be over with and rain.

And, now it finally had, the sun was new and foreign and blinding in an overwhelming way I couldn't explain. It felt good, warm on my skin and comforting. Yet, I couldn't fully open my eyes. They were sore from being shaded so long.

Because of this, my mother and I found we couldn't just sit and expose ourselves for long periods of time. We would both grow uncomfortable and shut down. So, we found a solution. During dinner we each allowed ourselves to ask one thing about each other to discuss. We had to answer and be one-hundred percent honest, but we got to choose how much was divulged.

It was a simple strategy, and it worked well for us. For the first time we spoke more than a couple sentences to each other a week. We actually talked-and I heard her laugh-really laugh-and it was the closest I'd ever felt to her. She didn't just feel like Meredith Sinclair, mayor of Ashwood Creek, anymore. She felt like Mom-not the home-makery type, or the soccer mom type, or the working mom type-but someone I could relate to, someone who was more than just surface level.

Things were changing and everyone noticed. My eyes were clear, my heart was open, and I felt like free falling.

"So, where is he?" Quinn sat perched on the arm of the chair opposite of mine, the one Bash usually fell into after dropping a new book in my lap.

I glanced down the aisle, listening for the book cart that never used to squeak but had started to recently. All I got was a whiff of dust and yellowing pages. We'd been sitting here for fifteen minutes, and still, there was no sign of Bash anywhere. It never took him this long to appear.

I shrugged. "Don't know. He usually senses I'm here. Maybe he took the day off."

A part of me was happy he hadn't shown. I didn't want to bring Quinn with me, but she insisted she get to meet Bash again since the last time she saw him was an embarrassing memory for me, to say the least.

I didn't want to share Bash with Quinn. She was always bubbly and flirty around guys, like her personality suddenly got dipped in sugar when one entered the room. And, maybe it was ridiculous to feel possessive of Bash because of my best friend, but I'd worked so hard to make sure Bash was my haven, my special person. I hated the idea of tainting that.

Quinn sighed and slipped down into the cushions boredly. After a moment of inspecting the ends of her dirty blonde hair, she looked up at me. "Can I be honest with you?"

I hated that question. It always made my insides seize up in panic. Nevertheless, I calmly answered, "Sure."

Her lips pursed. "He's not as cute as I thought he'd be."

The relief I felt made me giggle. "Oh?"

She nodded and then leaned across the end table between us to whisper, "He looks like one of our forefathers with that hair, don't you think? And, he works here, in the library? Shouldn't he be at a university?"

My face flushed, and I struggled to gather a coherent sentence when I heard a newly familiar squeaking sound and turned to see Bash rounding the corner. Seeing me, his lips stretched into a smile.

"Jovial," he crowed, "Now, what on Earth are you doing here? I thought I wasn't going to see you until this weekend -Oh...Hi." Bash stopped rolling the cart forward, and looked to Quinn.

My eyebrows pinched, and I looked behind me to see Quinn waving, a bit guiltily like she hadn't just been saying he looked like a forefather. I shook my head and turned to watch Bash slowly make the rest of the way over.

He pointed at her, and his forehead crinkled thoughtfully. "You're..."

"Quinn. Quinn Alberstein, Jovie's best friend," she answered.

"She wanted to come see you," I explained. "She's been begging since she found out about you that she get to see the guy that-"

"Makes her so happy," Quinn interrupted, smiling. My face warmed, but she continued, her cheeks glowing and her crossed leg swinging. "And, I didn't tell Jovie, but, I wanted to thank you-that's all. Some really good stuff has happened since you waltzed in. And, she'll never admit that she needs other people, but, I think she needed you."

I scowled, embarrassed. "Quinn."

Her smile grew wider, and she gave Bash a wink. "See?"

Bash stood there silently, lips turned up, eyes soft on me. My cheeks burned so much one might have thought I'd just stepped in from the cold. It wasn't untrue, but it wasn't something I ever wanted said out loud, either. And, having Quinn as an audience to Bash's fond gaze made a nervous flutter ripple through me and force my eyes to the floor. Then, he was at my side, pressing a kiss to my hair and thanking Quinn.

"She's very fortunate to have you in her life," Bash said to Quinn cordially. "But, I'm only here because she wants me here-not because she needed me in any way."

It felt weird to be listening to this conversation, which felt as though it should be taking place without my presence. Feeling antsy, I suddenly stood.

"Well." I laughed nervously and slung my jacket over my shoulders. "You guys have had a proper meeting, now. That's all good. But, I can't stay any longer because dinners with my mother have become very important to me."

Quinn blinked a couple of times in confusion. "Jovie, it's only four."

"It's time to go," I insisted, grabbing her arm.

She stood, grabbing her coat in a rush as I began backing away from the scene. Bash still stood beside the arm chair, eyes wide, forehead still crinkled as he tried to register what was happening. I don't know why I was embarrassed, but the fuzziness in my brain wasn't letting me process anything I was doing. Something about the exchange made me very uncomfortable, and I just couldn't place what it was.

It was beyond me even as I waved to Bash. "I'll see you this weekend."

He didn't reply. He simply watched me do what he does best in the library: disappear.

My mother and I still prepared dinner the same way we always did. She chatted away about work while we bustled around the kitchen pulling drawers open, boiling water, cutting vegetables, and walking around each other in perfect synchronization. But, where the chatter usually died away as we sat down to eat, it was forced to continue.

I had already learned some things about my mother I didn't already know. I asked little things in the beginning like what she was like as a kid, and who her best friends were. The more I unfolded, the bolder I became. I got her to touch on the subject of her mother, but she only repeated the things I already knew. And, I guess that was okay. From what I knew from both Meredith and Henry, my grandmother wasn't the most pleasant of people.

Tonight, I planned to ask about Henry. She could say as little or as much as she wanted on my father, but I didn't want to hear the same old thing she always said.

As we sat at the table and began to dish ourselves up, she waited patiently for my question since it was my turn to go first. I waited for her to finish, but asked before she could take a bite.

"Did Henry ever take you out on a date?"

My mother lowered her spoon before it got to her mouth and tilted her chin. "Henry? That's what you want to talk about?"

Her voice sounded tired, not angry or guarded like I expected.

I nodded. "Henry respects that you never want to talk about it, so he never tells me anything either. And, I'm sure it's because you're trying to kill the idea of you two ever being together, but, Henry's my dad. I kinda want to know why."

Sighing, she set her spoon on her plate. Then, she crossed her arms atop the table and looked at me seriously. "I knew this was going to come up, I guess I was just hoping I could avoid it."

"Why?" I asked.

Her lips twitched into a sad smile. "Because he never gave me a reason to treat him the way that I do. And...I didn't want my own daughter judging me."

I mimicked her posture and returned the same serious look. "Maybe I don't want to make the same mistake."

She held my gaze for a moment, and then her eyes dropped to the table where our dinner remained untouched. "He did take me on a date. Just, not in the traditional sense."

I felt a flurry of excitement, as though I'd just found a prize at the bottom of a cereal box. "He did?"

She nodded. "After work we went for a drive and just talked." She smiled a little. "He stopped at the park and he turned the music up. We laid on the roof of his car talking and looking at the stars. We didn't know any constellations, we just made them up and laughed." As she talked, I watched a dreamy look glaze over her eyes, I watched her sink into the dining room chair at the memory. "And, when the laughter died down we just looked at each other and I couldn't re- member the last time anyone made me feel that special. We weren't allowed to date our coworkers, so we were being a little rebellious," she laughed, blushing. She looked ten years younger as she spoke. "Then, this Johnny Cash song came on, and he loves Johnny Cash, so we got off the roof and we danced in the park. And, when the song was over he kissed me. And, that's all it took." She shook her head and glanced up at me. I blinked, waiting for her to continue, and although she looked reluctant to finish the story, she took a deep breath and carried on.

"And then I was embarrassed," she told me. "And I knew that we'd get in trouble. So, I stopped talking to Henry be- cause I didn't want anyone to find out that anything had happened between us. But, when I found out I was pregnant, it was hard to keep to myself. And, Henry wanted to be in your life so...my job suffered a bit, and the only reason

I wasn't immediately fired for the affair was because I am good at my job. Henry is only allowed to be my assistant as long as he remains stagnant in his position."

My fingers twisted together timidly. "Did you love him?"

She averted her eyes. "He's your father, and he takes good care of you."

"That isn't what I asked," I said, feeling my pulse quicken, knowing that if she said she loved him once, or maybe even that she loved him still, it would change everything I've ever known about them.

"I loved him once," she said, repeating what he had said to her not that long ago, and it was like watching Jericho's wall tumble down, revealing everything that could have been. And, as soon as she said it she recaptured my gaze in a frightened kind of way. "But, he can't ever know that. You know Henry. He'd do something stupid."

I nodded, and slumped back in my chair to process what she'd just told me. Not so long ago I would have thought my mother incapable of loving someone, but now, all I could feel was warmth in my chest, and a strange sense of satisfaction. Perhaps romantic love wasn't as hard as I used to think. Maybe it really wasn't about willingness in the matter.

"So," she said after she'd taken a bite of her dinner and let me sit in silence for a moment. "What about Bash? How do you think that's going to play out?"

I froze in place, unprepared for the question, and still shaken from the exchange between him and Quinn earlier that day. I still hadn't figured out why it bothered me so much.

"I don't know," I said, and it was an honest answer. "I can't stay with him forever. It's unrealistic."

"But, you want to stay with him?" She guessed.

I didn't say anything. I hated that question, hated it. I just wanted to wait it out, deal with it when the time came. The more I thought about all of these questions, the harder they became to answer.

It used to be easy. I would say: "We're going to separate before I graduate," or, "He agreed a long time ago to let go when I say so." But, things had changed these past few months. Feelings had changed. And, answering that way wasn't so easy anymore. It was painful.

"What does he do now, stack books? Not very ambitious. Certainly not someone who would be able to pull their own weight in a serious relationship," my mother continued, her voice heavier than before, like a weight ready to knock down my walls.

"He took a couple college courses here and there, but he's been busy moving around, finding himself, working..." I tell her a bit defensively.

She raised her eyebrows in a fashion that told me she wasn't convinced. "Ah. Well, just remember. When it comes to relationships, you can't be willy-nilly about it, okay? Not like me. That's why I don't bother anymore. I can't trust my own judgment-"

"But, Henry-"

"Is wonderful," she said, but it wasn't in the same tone she'd used earlier while talking about him. Something had realigned inside her. "But it almost got me fired. Think about it, Jovie. Bash is wonderful, too. But, he moseys around, and he's not serious. You don't end up with every man you love."

I looked at the lock in her jaw and the sharpness of her stare, and I knew she was speaking the only truth she knew.

"It's not forever, Bash and I," I told her, stonily. "It was never supposed to be."

Chapter 18

Bash was too intuitive not to notice the hesitancy that was reintroduced to our relationship upon the mending of my relationship with Meredith. And, well, it would be silly to say I wasn't equally disappointed with myself. With my mother it was like standing on a newly restored rope bridge, even though I knew the foundation was sturdy, I still trapezed across it warily, clutching the railing as though any second it would snap. Bash stood on the other side nodding his reassurances while the voices in my head warned that if I rushed toward his embrace, I would fall.

I was infuriated with myself.

And, Bash...he was far too understanding-which only made me angrier.

"I don't get how you can be so content with all of this," I seethed as I paced back and forth across the snow laden bridge that connected the park grounds to the library.

Beneath us, the lazy, slow-moving creek had frozen, and if I searched hard enough, I could make out the Christmas decorations lining the lampposts out on the street.

I turned on my heel, nearly slipping on ice, and gripped the railing tightly with icy, mitten-clad hands. "I'm the worst girlfriend imaginable and you act as though I've been nothing but good times and smooth sailing. It's been nearly six months and you haven't changed."

He stood behind me leaning on the opposite rail with his arms crossed and his aviator sunglasses gleaming in the white light. He breathed evenly, clouds of breath getting lost in the frigid winter air, and he held himself in the same fashion he did when we met: relaxed and unoffended.

"You haven't changed either," he replied in his slow-melting chocolate voice that I loved so much but hated in this moment.

I turned to face him, brows furrowing. "That's bullshit."

"It's the truth," he said matter-of-factly. "You're still scared, you're still guarded, you still refuse to sink into what I have to offer." He shrugged and turned his face away. "You're still one-hundred-percent the Jovie I met and fell in love with."

"How can that not bother you?" I wondered a bit too loudly, feeling a frustrated burst of energy surge through my arms as they flailed about. "That I'm guarded, and scared, or whatever. You work at a library in Ashwood Creek and you stay with me even though I don't deserve you, at all. Don't you think there's something greater for you out there? Don't you want to write a book, or see the world, or find a girl who gives you everything?"

His fists clenched under his folded arms, and his brows lowered under the frames of his glasses. And, for some reason, it was a relief.

"Are you attempting to break up with me, again?" His voice turned rigid.

"No," I told him. "I don't want that. I just don't want to hold you back."

"Jovie..." His shoulders slumped, and he pinched the bridge of his nose. "I chose all of this for myself." He glanced up. "I love it all. I love weaving around aisles of books all day, and I love Ashwood Creek and its quiet, small town appeal, and I love you and all your eccentricities. I love Greg and his Cigarette Graveyard. I love Henry's charm and Meredith's distaste for me. I love that Quinn is your best friend. I love how much more I appreciate my family when I go home. I love that we're all still figuring ourselves out, and that nothing is certain." He paused and took a step forward, gathering my hands in his. "I love my life, Jovie. I love every part of it. Stop letting your mother's expectations cloud the truth about life: that it's different from person to person."

Just touching his hands thawed my frozen ones, and I glanced up at his wind burnt cheeks, wondering how he was always able to do the impossible. "I guess I just expect that you'll tire of me-that none of this is exciting enough for you. That I've got too many issues-"

He released my hands and pressed a finger to my lips. I couldn't see his eyes past his sunglasses, but I could feel his eyes shining on me, warming me up despite the frequent gusts of icy wind.

"I don't use the word love lightly. If I say I love something, you better believe my whole heart is in it. This fear you have, that you aren't good enough? It's a reflex. I know it is. You know why?" He paused, and I shook my head. "Because whenever we have a moment of closeness, you panic. You try to put space between us. And I know you don't want to get attached because this isn't forever-but it's okay to want something. It's okay to give yourself a break. It's okay...to love me."

He removed his sunglasses and his blues eyes met mine with a sincerity that was so rich I felt my knees weaken. I felt the anger lift from my shoulders, and I reached out for him to steady myself.

"You think I love you?" I said in barely a whisper.

"Maybe you don't," he countered, blinking away a lone snowflake. "But, it's okay if you want to. You can break my heart, Jovial, I've told you a hundred times that you can, but I won't break yours. I will do everything in my power to keep you from it."

"You might not feel the same way by the time this is over," I warned.

"You'll remind me," he said in a voice that was somewhere up in the clouds. "You and reality have a funny kind of understanding. It's the same kind of understanding I have with fate."

There was something about Bash. Maybe it was his voice, maybe it was his conviction, but he could get me choked up. He could get my insides to double knot, and my lungs to forget to fill, and my brain to go foggy. He could whisk me off to share a daydream.

Suddenly, it didn't quite matter what Meredith thought. She didn't understand what I did: that Bash and I knew each other perfectly-that we didn't need forever. We just needed now. And now was good.

I followed Bash into the new year feeling lighter than I'd felt in a long time. It was incomparable to anything I'd ever experienced. There had always been a heavy weight attached at my ankle keeping me from venturing out. And, sure, it lightened up here and there, but not quite like this. Now that weight felt like a helium balloon tied where a chain had been.

Things that had never been turned into a routine, and I gladly welcomed it. I went to school and gushed about Bash to Quinn, I ate dinner with Meredith and we actually talked, I spent the weekend with Henry and we watched the History Channel side-by-side until we fell asleep on the couch, and all the moments in between I spent with Bash. But, it wasn't quite like before.

I felt more open, now, like he had seen every inch of my soul. He knew my fears and I knew his. And, although it was terrifying at first, I was surprised to discover how fond I became of it. I always thought of my insides as Pandora's box. I never really liked it, but I accepted who it made me. But, sharing it with Bash, having somebody who truly knew me, who understood me on a different level than even Quinn made me realize that I was capable of more. I wasn't a machine, I wasn't my mother, I was something else entirely. I was human, I was real, and confiding in someone somehow made that whole idea tangible.

Bash wrote a lot. He seemed to always be writing. And, when he wasn't writing he was reading. His book of pretentious words was always cracked open, ready to be filled with the next moribund, propitious, or eleemosynary. I liked to watch him. I'd sit as his apartment doing homework just to be near him. And, if Henry let me get away with it, I liked staying the night. There's nothing lonelier than after midnight, and he always held me close.

Sometimes Greg was around, other times he was off doing whatever it is that he did. When he was around, the window above the Cigarette Graveyard would be open, turning the whole room cold until the stale smell of nicotine wafted out into the quiet streets of Ashwood Creek. He always had something snappy to say, and made a point of teasing Bash whenever the moment presented itself. And, funnily enough, I liked their little world of books, cigarettes, banter, and take-out.

Soon, the snow began to melt, and my neighbor's chickens began to squawk all hours of the day, again. Regardless, I sat outside on the steps before my mother's front door reading a book Bash recommended me in the yellow sunlight. And because Quinn possessed the radar-like ability to know I was out, it didn't take her long to appear in the front yard.

"Hey," she called to get my attention.

I glanced up where she stood with her light hair up and her dimpled smile crooked.

"Hey," I said back. She took it as an invitation to take a seat beside me on the creaky wooden steps. "Your birthday's coming up. The big eighteen."

She was much better at remembering things like that. I frequently had to be reminded of such events, but she always knew. She always remembered everything.

"Yep," I said, trying to push the idea from my mind. Things were going too good. I didn't need a reminder that the sand in the hourglass was slowly running out.

"Anything you've been wanting?" she asked. Her voice was high and clear, excited that by this time next week, we'd both be adults. When I glanced over, she flashed me a brilliant smile, and the arches of her brows became exaggerated.

I shrugged. "You don't have to get me anything, you know that. It's just a birthday."

"I know," she said, her knees bouncing. "But, I want to. So, is there anything you've been dying to get your hands on?"

I felt like I had everything. There wasn't a thing in the world I wanted more than time, but I wouldn't let myself sink into that pit. I spent far too long looking toward a future that didn't exist, yet. I wanted to continue living in the moment that would turn out to be one of the best chapters in my life thus far.

"A leather bound journal," I said, suddenly.

"Journal? Really, that's what you want?" she asked, unconvinced. Her knees stopped bouncing and she propped her chin up in her hand. "You sure?"

I nodded without even realizing it.

"Yes," I answered after a moment of silence. "That's all I want."

"Well, okay," she sang.

Across the street, the old man who sang show tunes was pulling his old rocking chair out onto the porch. Quinn and I watched as he made himself comfortable atop the cushions. It was still too early for him to obsess over de-podding vegetables, so he sat across from us with the day's newspaper opened in his lap, pen at the ready over the crossword puzzle. Then, ever-so-softly, he began to sing.

Quinn and I glanced at each other and giggled. Spring was officially here.

Chapter 19

Johnny Cash played quietly from the kitchen where Henry washed cake crumbs off of mismatched plates. I was just around the corner curled into the cushions of the pullout sofa admiring the gifts I'd received.

I was happy to have my birthday done and over with. I never liked much fussing over that kind of thing, but I put up with it every year all the same. I usually received the same thing from Meredith every year. She would fill a box with sensible things that she knew I'd use—which I preferred to knickknacks and trinkets. But, this year she surprised me with a very grown-up dress for graduation that looked tailored and sophisticated enough to wear for years to come. She matched it with a necklace fitted with my birthstone: aquamarine.

Henry, on the other hand, was never sensible. He was the giver of trinkets and knickknacks that never had any real use—other than the bike he gave me a couple years ago. And, this year, he lived up to the expectation by giving me a picture book. I shook my head, smiling fondly at it. I'd only looked through it briefly when Henry gave it to me.

Now, I flipped it open to the first page, and my eyes softened on a rare baby picture of him holding me in the hospital. He looked pretty much the same, although his hair was lighter and his skin glowing in a way only youth can provide, and he held me close, looking down with a smile. Alongside the picture was an annotation that read: Eighteen years ago Meredith called me from the hospital saying you'd finally decided to join us in this world. And when I held you for the first time, I fell in love. Meredith wanted to call you Lauren—something simple—but I wanted something fresher, something new, something you could define. And, on that one rare occasion, I got Meredith to change her mind. I asked how she felt when she looked at you for the first time, and her smile was one I can never forget. She said "happy." But, of course, we couldn't call you that. So, we called you Jovie, and you've been surprising me ever since.

My chest tightened as I read it, and I felt my eyes water just enough that it turned his handwriting into a blur. I blinked it away quickly, not wanting Henry to see that I was getting emotional. He'd been a bit keener about that these days. He noticed I was floating on the edge of a daydream as I fell deeper for Bash, and he always wanted to talk about feelings. But, I still felt uncomfortable sharing too much of it with him and Meredith, and I would immediately change the subject. Nevertheless, he'd still prod for something else, search for some other vulnerability that would prompt a similar conversation. It was exhausting.

Nevertheless, warmth settled around me like a hug when I read his message. I had never once heard the story of how I got my name before, and somehow knowing it made me flush with pride and admiration. I felt...special.

I turned the page where he'd turned some cards into a collage, all of them congratulating him and Meredith on my birth. There was even a newspaper clipping that seemed to ignore all the politics of my existence and focused on the miracle of new life with a happy little blurb about my family. I continued to smile as I turned the page, again.

The water stopped running in the kitchen, and the clattering about of dishes faded until finally Henry rounded the corner wiping his hands on his jeans. He noticed the book open in my lap and met my eyes nervously—like he was unsure about his gift.

"What do you think?"

I knew I was smiling, but I wasn't expecting myself to suddenly stand and hug him—but I did.

"It's amazing. Where did you find the time to do this?"

He squeezed me back equally as tight, but I felt him shrug. "I've been working on it for a couple of years."

I released him and took a step back, staring up in awe. I knew Henry was crafty, he had the old art projects to prove it, but I hadn't pegged him as a particularly "scrap-booky" type person.

"How is it that I've known you and Mom all of my life and yet I hardly know you," I wondered in amazement. "Lately it feels like every day I'm going to be greeted with a new surprise."

He laughed and placed a comforting hand on my shoulder. "I think part of growing up—for both the kid and the parents—is realizing that there's more than what meets the eye. You start to see each other as equals, as people."

I nodded, knowing with every fiber of my being that it was a true statement. The struggle I had with my mother a few months ago made sense for, yet, another reason.

I hardly ever called Henry anything other than his name, but this time it felt appropriate to use a word I hardly ever broke out.

"I love you, Dad."

A flicker of realization flashed across his eyes when he heard me say it. I smiled meekly and continued to do so even as he scooped me back up into his arms.

"Love you too, Jo-Jo," he mumbled into my hair, and I knew his emotional side, the one true defining thing about him, was taking control as he held me as close as he did when I was a newborn.

Bash and I went on our first bike ride of the year under a deep blue sky with the stars twinkling like jewels and the moon bright and full. He followed behind me lazily, looking up at the unobstructed view with large, clear eyes. The wind pulled strands of gold hair from a loosely constructed bun at the back of his head—his hair was long enough to do that now. I meandered my way across empty streets and over bumps of cracked sidewalk fluidly, listening to the rattle of the bike chain in the quiet of the sleepy neighborhood outside his apartment.

"The world feels very paradisiacal this time of night, don't you agree?" he asked as we neared the edge of the neighborhood and it opened into countryside that was thinly spread with homes. From out here you could really smell the damp earth from the melted snow and not just wet gravel and car exhaust. Somebody's wind chime jingled with a short breeze. Only the lights from people's bedroom windows indicated the world was not quite asleep yet, but still, it was growing lethargic. Perhaps it was merely yawning.

I took my feet off the peddles and slowed to roll alongside him. The air was very damp, as it usually is in the spring when the world can't seem to keep the earth wet enough. It wasn't a cold damp, though. It was a sticky one, and I lifted the hair from my neck with one hand and glanced at Bash.

"You think that about everything."

His eyes stayed focused on the wild grass beside the road. "No, there's a different word for different times of the day."

I laughed lightly. "But they're all adjectives of one another."

He shrugged. "They have their nuances."

I shook my head, but I was grinning at his stubbornness.

He looked to me suddenly, the angles of his face catching the moonlight in a fantastical kind of way that I enjoyed. He always looked like art, somehow.

"Have you decided?"

He tried to look at me directly as he asked, but I turned my eyes toward the uneven pavement before he could finish.

Bash had been almost as obsessive about the question as my mother, and I couldn't figure out why. He had no reason to bother with wanting to know where I'd end up going to school—he wasn't a part of that path, and I hated thinking about it. But, he knew, just like everyone knew, that I'd decided and I was simply keeping it to myself, holding off on the finality of it all.

"Bash..."

"Jovie," he countered, determination balancing on his cheekbones and reflecting in his eyes.

Maybe that was the reason he suggested we do this, so that he could ask without me making an excuse that I had to leave. I sighed heavily, squeezing my eyes shut.

"Why is it so important to you?" I asked, refusing the question with a distraction, but also curious.

He stopped peddling and placed a foot on the ground, stopping his forward motion so that I had to stop, too. He turned his face to the stars and took a deep breath of damp air.

"I love you, that's all," he answered in a defeated voice.

I watched his eye lashes flutter and his aloof posture stutter, and I sunk back onto the seat of my bike with a frown.

"You know it's not possible to continue being together after I graduate," I said carefully in a small voice. Even then I worried I'd shatter something fragile in him. Still, my words made even my heart throb painfully.

To my surprise, he simply nodded, but his hands seem to grip the handles of his bike a bit harder. "I know, I just..."

He didn't finish.

The air between us turned tense, and I knew I had to say something, had to reveal something to him to make him understand that this wasn't easy for me, either.

"I wish it could," I told him softly. "But, no matter what happens here in Ashwood Creek, I need to go out and be with myself. It's a journey I have to do alone—and I don't want to hold you back, or drag you along with me...ever. Things are perfect now, but..."

"That could change?" he guessed, his smile small and crooked.

"You have my heart," I assured him, and his eyes seemed to twinkle like the stars. "But we're both still figuring everything out."

He folded his hands together in his lap and looked at me, nodding. "I understand, Jovial. Really, I do. It's just hard to imagine an expiration date when all I want is forever. Except, we both know it's not possible." He shook his head. "It is truly the quirkiest relationship I've ever been in. And, funnily enough, it's the one I crave most."

"It's like laughing when you're told not to," I provided, understanding completely what he was getting at.

"Exactly."

We laughed a little, nodding and staring off somewhere that wasn't into each other's souls. The sky had grown unbelievably dark in the past couple of minutes and lights had gone out in many homes. I could no longer make out the features of Bash's face. So, I told him.

"New York. In Manhattan. There's a university there that's given me an academic scholarship, and it's the smartest route to take."

"I'm proud of you."

He didn't comment on the distance—how it really wasn't all that far. He didn't comment on the big city—the kind of big city he had run from that I was running toward. He didn't' try to say anything at all. Just that he was proud, and that was everything I needed.

There wasn't much space between us, so I tipped off my bike and leaned toward him, standing on my tiptoe to press a kiss to his cheek.

He turned his face toward me, his eyes adjusting to the dark and the shadowy effect it had on my features. His eyes searched mine, looking for something I didn't know if he found or not, but he still kissed me all the same, lowering himself off his bike and pressing me close to him. These days when he kissed me it felt like tossing back liquor. The more of it I had, the easier it became to block the rest of the world out, to feel only him and taste chamomile tea on his lips and smell amber on his skin.

He was paradisiacal, and I hardly think he ever knew it. I wanted him to believe it, though. I still do.

Chapter 20

April 17th, 2013

She broke my heart.

I wish she would have told me what this relationship meant to her. I wish she would have told me this was a relationship made out of ice, floating in a sea of warm water, everyday growing closer to being nothing. She knew she wasn't going to stay—so why did she say it? Why did she announce she loved me? Why did she kiss me goodbye?

She must be a damn good actress. She can breathe "I love you" like the best of them.

But, I worry now—Does she understand what it means?

I love you does not mean I'm secretly planning to leave you after I've had my fun. I love you does not mean getting bored and keeping others close behind. I love you doesn't mean "you were just a placeholder."

I love you is an ache in your bones. It's the catch in your breath like you've run a marathon, and nervous laughter as you undress them for the first time. It's trust. It's loyalty. It's lipstick stains on necks, and your cologne on their clothes. It's jumping off a swing and swimming in the deep end. I love you is their hand in yours. It's falling down and then standing back up. It's hanging over a cliff knowing that if you can't pull yourself up, they'll be there to help you. It's intense. It's real. It's chemical.

And, it doesn't have to mean forever, but it sure as hell should mean I'm the only one you're thinking about.

I've never really been in love before. This was the first. She knew she was my first. She knew she was in control.

I shouldn't have given her control.

My head hurts. Everything feels like it's throbbing. And, I hate how this feels. I hate the salty taste of tears. I hate how she did this to me. But I don't hate one thing.

I don't hate that I feel everything. I feel it all. This experience has opened my eyes.

Dear future Bash, if you are ever to fall in love again, fall in love with someone honest. Fall in love with someone who doesn't keep you guessing what their next step is going to be. Fall in love with a girl who tells you how it's going to end. And, when she breaks your heart, perhaps you will feel this all again. And maybe, just maybe, you can do something about it.

Signed,

Bash Daley

I flipped the leather bound journal over in my hands, feeling the soft cover and breathing in the new book smell. Quinn had wrapped it in nothing but a bow for my birthday, and though that felt like ages ago, I hadn't really looked at it since. I didn't know what I was going to do with it yet, but something told me that I needed it, that it'd somehow become useful. I did bottle things up, after all. I might have suggested I have one because that needed to stop. Then again, maybe I was inspired by Bash and his grandfather.

It was sort of daunting, all of those blank pages. I didn't think I'd be able to fill them all. Bash had filled up stacks of composition notebooks with his thoughts, but, well, he was articulate.

I fell back onto my mattress, holding the journal above my face with a narrowed, calculating stare at the smooth, leather cover.

It'll come to you, I thought. You'll find something to do with it.

Greg sat in the open window of his and Bash's apartment with a lit cigarette and a painfully old Leonard Cohen track playing from the stereo. Bash and I sat on the living room couch with his head in my lap as he quizzed me on enzyme inhibition for my upcoming biology test.

I rocked my head back boredly while Bash babbled on about an answer I gave that needed elaboration.

"Alright, so, moving on," he continued, not caring that I was barely paying attention to anything he'd been discussing. "What is the difference between competitive and non-competitive inhibition?"

I resisted a groan, but Greg didn't. Usually he was more aloof than Bash and smoked quietly, unperturbed. Today was not one of those days.

"Jesus Christ," Greg all but snapped. "This has been going on for the past hour. Don't you people ever do anything normal?"

"This is perfectly normal, Gregory," Bash hummed. He folded my answer sheet onto his chest and looked up at the ceiling. "You don't have to sit there and listen."

"Oh, but I do," Greg grumbled. "Every time she's here you two sit around mulling over books and papers and homework. God, if this is what dating a high schooler looks like—I feel sorry for you."

Bash sighed. "Put out your cigarette and take a walk, then."

"No!" Greg huffed stubbornly and dragged on his cigarette extra-long. "This is my house, too."

"You're being a child," I told him, patience running thin. My head hurt from breathing in second-hand smoke and studying all afternoon. Not to mention his music taste was absolutely god awful.

"I do not remember high school this way," Greg continued pointedly, preparing himself for a rant. "I remember getting my first girlfriend, my first job, having my first beer, attending parties, going to prom. What the hell. It hasn't been that long since I've been out and they've turned the place into an intellectual prison."

"No, you just didn't try," I guessed and tossed a glance over the couch. "Some of us are trying to get college credit while it doesn't break the bank."

He scoffed and hid behind his cigarette, but he didn't argue. He simply allowed himself to reblend into the background, muttering quietly under his breath.

Releasing my frustration with a heavy sigh, I glanced down at Bash's face, his lips curling up in a humorous grin.

"You're awful acrimonious today," he commented lightly, eyebrows lifting like he'd finally discovered the answer to a long, unanswered question.

And, well, maybe he was right. I was stressed and bitter from all the extra work I had been doing as an advanced student. It felt like I was constantly weighted down by school work these days. If it wasn't a project, it was a paper, and if it wasn't a paper, it was a four page assignment.

Most of my time with Bash was turning into study dates. That made me feel horrible because I didn't want to burden him with that. He graduated years ago.

Still, he kept insisting we do it together because otherwise we would hardly see each other. If he wasn't quizzing or listening to me while we sat in his apartment, he was doing it while stacking books. And that wasn't right.

He was good to me. Too good. And, while I had known that all along, it was really sinking in, now.

"Sorry," I told him dismissively. "I'm just tired. It's fine. Keep going."

Bash sat up and tossed the answer sheet onto the messy coffee table. I could tell by his sudden burst of energy that continuing with the study prep wasn't going to happen.

"No, maybe Greg is right."

"—oh, really? No way. I'm so surprised by this, Sebastian. Me? Right about something?" Greg moved the cigarette from his face and caught my eye with his dull ones. "It's been known to happen. Quite often."

I tried to glare, but Bash started to speak, again.

"Come on, Jovial. I haven't seen that ethereal smile of yours in ages." He looked at me earnestly, and it became obvious to me that all of this studying really was taking a toll on him, too.

I could feel the tension in my own shoulders like an annoying pinch. And, as far as I could tell, I might have been sleepwalking these past weeks. While everyone else was perking up because of spring, I was losing my glow. I knew I needed a break, I was just afraid of taking one.

But, with Bash's eyes shining on me the way that they were, lighting me up like the sun, I knew that if he thought I needed a break, then now was the time to take one.

"Okay...fine," I conceded. "We're done for the day. What do you want to do?"

"I'm leaving!" Greg announced suddenly, jumping off the window sill and dropping his cigarette into its grave. Both Bash and I turned to watch as he placed the board on top of the flowerbox and pushed the window into place. "I don't want to be around when this gets weird."

And, with that, he powerwalked into his bedroom and shut the door. Bash and I glanced at each other with wide eyes. I knew my face was burning, but he just looked genuinely confused. It was after a few moments of silence that I realized that it wasn't, in fact, so silent.

"He left that shitty music on," I groaned in annoyance.

Bash's mouth dropped open in disgust of my comment. "Shitty music? Jovial, Leonard Cohen is a true artist."

"You like this stuff, too?" I asked and wrinkled my nose. "Really, Bash?"

Bash waved his hands, having none of it. "Jovial, this man writes of love and purpose in a poetic, compelling rhythm that speaks to the soul!"

"Well, that just sounded hopeless and cheesy," I told him dryly as I smoothed out the place on my jeans where he'd been lying, demonstrating my lack of interest.

He slapped his hands over his face in disbelief.

"No," he stated simply, standing up. "No girlfriend of mine lacks appreciation for Leonard Cohen."

With that, he grabbed my hands and pulled me off the couch, dragging me out to a bare piece of flooring that was just wide enough for both of us to stand with our arms out. I glanced around in confusion, but he took my hand and held it over my head, twisting so I spun before him.

"This is even my favorite song of his," Bash announced as the next track lined up, and if I thought his talking voice was sweet and rich in a way I couldn't describe, his singing voice was twice as wonderful.

"Well I've heard there was a secret chord that David played and it pleased the Lord, but you don't really care for music, do you?" His eyes gleamed as he sang along lowly, rocking me back and forth to the steady sing-talking that was Leonard Cohen's voice. "Well it goes like this: the fourth, the fifth, the minor fall and the major lift, the baffled king composing Hallelujah..."

His arms circled my waist, pulling me close and singing into my hair. I smelled the fresh linen on his clothing, and leaned in closer while his mouth lowered to my ear to sing in a slightly husky, stomach churning voice that gave me second thoughts about what I'd said earlier.

And, I guess that was Bash's charm—always making me second guess myself.

"Well your faith was strong but you needed proof. You saw her bathing on the roof. Her beauty and the moonlight overthrew ya." Bash took one of my hands and guided it to his shoulder while he took my waist and held our other hands out to lead. We began to shuffle in a small circle while the song played on. "She tied you to her kitchen chair, she broke your throne, and she cut your hair, and from your lips she drew the Hallelujah..."

His eyes closed, and his body relaxed as he sunk into the song. I looked up, watching his lips move with the lyrics, skin tingling where he held my waist and goosebumps dancing down my spine. The background melted into nothingness. Heat built up beneath my skin.

In a way, I felt like Bash was singing about me--as silly as that was. It was just a song, but when he looked at me, it didn't feel that simple. My final wall went down.

His voice softened with the singer's, and I pressed myself closer against him. "I did my best, it wasn't much. I couldn't feel, so I tried to touch. I've told the truth, I didn't come to fool you. And even though it all went wrong I'll stand before the Lord of Song with nothing on my tongue but Hallelujah..."

And, on his intake of breath, I stopped our slow dancing and stood on my tiptoes to press my lips against his. He dropped my hand and gripped behind my neck, pulling me closer, kissing me deeper, and I felt all of the tension in my body, all the worries in my mind erase with every caress of his lips.

"Hallelujah," I breathed against his mouth.

He grinned and pushed the hair from my face, moving forward to kiss me again.

I love you is an ache in your bones. It's the catch in your breath like you've run a marathon, and nervous laughter as you undress them for the first time. It's trust. It's loyalty. It's lipstick stains on necks, and your cologne on their clothes. It's jumping off a swing and swimming in the deep end. I love you is their hand in yours. It's falling down and then standing back up. It's hanging over a cliff knowing that if you can't pull yourself up, they'll be there to help you. It's intense. It's real. It's chemical.

As our kiss broke, I said it again. "Hallelujah."

I'm not brave enough to say I love you.

Chapter 21

They say that people change over time. They say that when push comes to shove people can do the unexpected. I always thought that the change they were talking about would be groundbreaking, that all of a sudden somebody would wake up completely different from the person they had been before.

I was wrong. And, I guess that's why people seemed constant to me for the longest time.

It's gradual, like the way the ocean waves polish rocks along the shore. We forget that as we're changing and growing, so are the people around us. Maybe they're in sync, being altered by life the same way we are. Similarities and differences in experiences leave nuances in behaviors, so much or so little that we hardly ever notice or we suddenly start to drift.

I didn't notice how much the people in my life had changed in the past year until I lied in an unfamiliar bed in a Manhattan dorm room swallowed by the dark, unable to sleep.

It was just a tour, just a weekend stay at the university I would be attending in the fall. Meredith had made the seven hour trip with me, an impossible feat I thought I'd never witness, and left me uneasy and nervous in a crowd of high school seniors I may see on campus later that year.

I didn't think of myself as a shy person, I could get my way through uncomfortable situations just fine. In fact, this is an experience I had looked forward to my whole life, to be able to step into a crowd of unfamiliar faces and become invisible. But, as I made my way through the crowd to register, I found myself feeling lonely and lost.

And, while there were fun moments in the tour and good laughs with the girl whose dorm I was staying in, I began to get homesick. I began to miss the people I thought would be easy to say goodbye to-and I'd been there less than twenty-four hours.

That terrified me. I wondered what had happened to me, what I had done to make myself so vulnerable to change and new atmospheres.

Here I was these past months pushing for a relationship with my mother I never thought I would have. Here I had been falling in love. Here I had been establishing an identity in entirely the wrong place. That wasn't supposed to happen until after I'd left Ashwood Creek so that I could start fresh and make my own rules. I wasn't supposed to bring baggage-just snip the ties and find myself.

It felt awful disappointing lying in a bed that was too springy with my eyes trained on the grey ceiling, melting it into a void of my own insecurities as they flashed before my eyes. It was so confusing to want to hate something that you loved. It felt wrong to want to let go of Ashwood Creek.

I'd grown far too attached to perishable things.

I just wanted to numb the stabbing in my gut and clamp my hands over my ears to stop the little voice in the back of my head from telling me all the things I was afraid of hearing. I wanted to stop feeling so much.

And even though at home, in Ashwood Creek, I was happier than I had ever been, deep down inside I wished that I had never changed. I begged the ocean to stop rolling over the shore.

I knew in the beginning that staying attached to things would do this, but I also told myself that I could end it all without so much as a frown.

I was wrong. I was so wrong.

As I listened to my roommate snore, I decided that I didn't regret these past couple of months. I only wished it hadn't affected me with this much intensity because saying goodbye would sting like a slap across the cheek-or like a permanent ache in a once impenetrable heart.

I knew there was nothing left for me to hold back anymore because it would all hurt the same way in the end. All the work I did to protect myself had been in vain.

Like everyone else, I drove back home with my mother thinking about what the future held. Where there used to be solid ideas now stood a vast arena of obstacles I did not prepare for.

"Did you ever feel unprepared?" I asked Meredith as I watched the ever-changing landscape fly past. My fingers twisted in my lap tightly, turning the knuckles white.

"I knew what I wanted the final product to look like," she told me, her eyes trained on the road ahead of her. "That's the best you can do."

I glanced at her anxiously, watching the dark baby hairs near her face be blasted back by the fans of the air conditioning, and her chin lower from its usual authoritative pose. She looked over, catching the panic in the reflection of my eyes.

Her hand twitched on the steering wheel, trying to decide, and then suddenly she reached over and placed it over my knotted ones. "You're going to be fine. I raised you."

When I saw Bash next, the librarian at the upstairs reception desk yelled at me for running in the building. And, well, I wasn't actually running, so I didn't really deserve that scolding as I jogged past her and began weaving through bookshelves until the faint squealing of the book cart forced me to a halt and Bash's chocolate melting voice was in my ears.

"Jovial?"

I turned on my toes, finding him leaning over the book cart in confusion.

I can't explain what made me do it, can't possibly begin to dissect what was going on in my head when I bounced down the aisle and threw myself at him with so much force that he backed into the adult romance bookshelf and knocked down a few novels.

"Whoa, whoa, whoa-"

Holding his face close, I stood on tip toes to silence him with my lips.

He responded hesitantly, kissing me back lightly until he pulled his face back and gazed down with a puzzled expression.

"What is in the air in Manhattan? I just fixed this shelf... "

I lowered myself onto flat feet and looked down at the mess I made, wincing. "I'm sorry. I just...missed you."

I watched as the expression on his face morphed from bewilderment to a genuine breathlessness that only his face could illustrate so perfectly. His eyes hooded for a brief moment before closing completely and recapturing my lips, kissing me softer than before and with a certain kind of beautiful, romantic honesty that can only be felt when people are in love.

It wasn't until he was backing me up against the opposite bookshelf that either of us remembered how very publically we were displaying our affection-especially in his place of employment.

He pulled back slowly, and I noticed that, like mine, his cheeks were a burning hue of crimson. He laughed at himself and buried his face into his shoulder.

"Sorry."

My hands were on his shoulders, eyes watching him flush and stutter about the same way he always did when he was embarrassed. A smile stretched across my face as I watched him back up and duck down to collect the fallen books.

"I'm sorry," I told him, bending down to help him. "That was me. You're working, I shouldn't have."

I helped him line the books back across the shelf. When we finished, he swiped his thumb across his bottom lip and smiled at me.

After a moment of us standing passion-charged in the deserted romance section of the library, he confidently stated, "You never say it, but you do."

"What's that?" I asked, feeling my breath catch in anticipation of what I knew he was going to say.

"I love you."

My heart hurt as it hammered in my chest, because despite all the things I could say, those three words never tumbled out. So, I tried a different combination of words.

"Well, I do."

He caught a length of my hair between his fingers and tucked it behind my ear, watching my heavy gaze. He could make me feel like I was melting into the floor or flying as high as a bird when he looked back at me that way. "I know."

I helped Bash finish up at work. We went into the office and finished collecting returned books, he ran the front desk while the other librarian took her lunch break, and he pulled me into deserted aisles to steal a kiss when he thought none of the librarians would notice. But, when he grabbed his coat from the back room, the lady behind the desk winked at me, and I knew that everyone here knew more than they let on.

It was late afternoon when we left and headed back to his apartment. Sunday never felt more threatening and peaceful all at once. I knew I would have to be back at Henry's before the night got too late, but I was determined to be with Bash as long as I could tonight.

"Greg won't be back until later. He's out with work friends, I guess," Bash told me as we entered his dark apartment. The nicotine smell was always faint to none when Greg was out.

That meant that when I stood next to Bash in the tiny entryway, I could smell only amber and detergent and dust from old books. Something felt very different about being alone with Bash today, something exciting that made my insides feel like cotton.

He shrugged out of his jacket and helped me out of mine, but the lights were still out and when he turned back around, he crowded me back against the wall-whether on accident, or on purpose, I don't know, but it made pulling him forward by his shirt easier.

His lips met mine with an intake of breath, and he fell forward, pressing a forearm against the wall beside my face to support himself. I felt him take a step forward between kisses, pressing closer to me so that I could feel his body against mine.

My head was spinning as he ducked his head down, tracing my jaw with his lips and pressing kisses down my neck. I opened my eyes to watch a bead of light slip between the door and the floor, tracing a broken pattern across the scuffed floor. My skin was warm, and every kiss he pressed to my neck felt like fire.

Smoothing my hair back, he brought himself back to eye level. My lips parted in anticipation, but he simply brushed his nose against mine and looked me in the eye.

"Hi," he whispered lowly, his lips pulling into a grin.

I felt as though I could run a marathon or jump off the highest cliff into the ocean below, but none of that could compare to the kind of adrenaline I felt coursing through my veins.

I barely managed to say it back. My eyes were too busy being drawn to his and my fingers too occupied tracing the edge of one of the buttons on his shirt.

"Tell me what you're feeling," he queried, his voice much lower than I was used to.

I shifted against the wall, knowing I'd made up my mind.

"While I was in Manhattan I realized that I shouldn't be wasting my time with you-it's too precious. I don't want to regret not putting everything I have into this relationship, Bash. You're a very particular kind of feeling. Nobody else will ever make me feel the way that you do..." He lowered his forehead to rest on my shoulder, and I thought I would collapse from the electricity that jolted within me. "I feel like now is perfect. Everything is perfect."

"Even though this isn't forever?"

I tugged lightly at the back of his hair so that he'd look up. "Is that okay?"

The shadows on his face and his long hair made his expression hard to read. "It's okay," he finally answered. "I love you."

I craned forward until our lips met again, and then it all fell into place. My fingers undid the buttons of his shirt and rolled the fabric off his shoulders. He unhooked my bra and I pulled it out of my sleeve, dropping it to the floor beside our bare feet. I could focus on nothing else but the sound of our breath, the pulling apart of lips, and the sound of clothing hitting the floor as we stumbled into his bedroom.

Bash's curtains were open, allowing moonlight to illuminate our bare skin in the otherwise dark and silent bedroom. I ached a little, but watching him trace the lines of my open palm with his fingers distracted me enough that I didn't mind.

Sex isn't how they make it look in the movies. There's awkward giggles and moments where everything is completely out of sync. Sweat drips from foreheads. Someone slips or holds their breath or pulls the sheets until they unhook from the mattress. And, yes, it's a little weird.

But, tossed in with that weirdness is a blend of real emotion: trust, desire, love, wholeness.

Bash kissed my shoulder and wrapped me closer against him. With his chest against my back, I could feel our hearts beat together.

"Are you okay?"

He was using the simplest words he knew all day, and I was grateful for that because there's something to be said about easy, unembellished conversation: it's often times more powerful.

I looked over my shoulder. "I'm more than okay."

His hands wrapped against mine and squeezed tightly.

I always thought I would regret something like sex. Maybe it's because I was an accident. But, I never regretted this.

We were deeply in love, and that's all that mattered.

Chapter 22

"So, that's it? It's Manhattan for sure?" Quinn crossed her arms and fell back against her bedsheets with a frown.

I propped myself up on an elbow and nodded. "I told you I didn't plan on staying here."

She stared up at the ceiling and pursed her lips. "I just thought you'd change your mind after Meredith. I thought you would decide to stay in state. I'm staying in state. What am I gonna do without you? You're, like, my sister."

I sighed and lowered my gaze to the floral design of her bedsheets. When I decided I was going to tell Quinn about Manhattan, I didn't expect a twist in my gut to follow, or for dread to cloud the parts of my brain that tried to make sense of everything. I also didn't think she would be so put out by the news. She knew I wasn't one to change my mind so easily.

"And, you're like mine," I told her, hoping the statement would take away from the sting. "But, I'm really serious about starting fresh. I always have been. That doesn't mean I'm not going to come back here. I do want to continue a relationship with my mom. Plus, you know, there's Henry."

"And Bash?" She asked, turning her head to watch my reaction.

That question had come to make my insides feel like sludge. Quinn watched as my face fell. With a heavy sigh, I rolled onto my back.

"It's not realistic."

She reached across to place a light hand on my upper arm. "Does he know?"

I nodded.

"He's so good for you, Jovie—"

"I know," I cut in, pulling my arm out from under her hand. "But, it's not fair to him. He deserves better. I don't want to pull him along while I try to figure out my life."

"You love him," she guessed quietly. She knew me entirely too well.

"This isn't about running away from feelings, or being bored, or walking away because he doesn't do anything for me anymore. It's not about finding the easiest path to follow." I wrapped my arms around myself and turned my head away from Quinn. "It's about giving each other our best shot."

Quinn let out a deep breath and sat back up. "Well, if it's meant to be, you'll find a way back to each other when you're ready."

Unsure of how to respond, I slowly pulled myself back up to a sitting position as well.

"You always say the right stuff," I told her, bumping my knee against hers. "I couldn't ask for a better sister."

Her lips pulled into a gentle smile and she grabbed my shoulder, looking serious. "Promise you won't forget me?"

I leaned over and wrapped my arms over her shoulders, smiling when she squeezed me back. "Promise. I know you'll give me an earful if I don't call."

She giggled and leaned back. "Damn right I will."

Time seemed to come and go too quickly. It was as if it knew I was having trouble keeping up. We were all free-falling, and suddenly I had to choose what to hold on to. There was only so much time before we'd crash back into reality and I only had two hands. I couldn't grab for the things I wanted. I had to grab for what I needed. That's the only way I'd make it out in one piece.

To make up for what I knew what was coming, I put everything I had into the last moments of my life with Bash. Both Meredith and Henry seemed to understand, and not much was said when I would miss curfew to be with Bash. We would bike through town, and read to each other, and slow dance to Leonard Cohen. We would laugh at bad jokes, leave sticky notes in books, eat takeout on the weekends, and fall asleep listening to a thunderstorm.

He truly had become my haven.

"I don't say it enough," I told him one day while we sat together at our spot in the library, both wedged tightly into the same leather chair. "But, I like the way your voice sounds, and that you smell like home. I like when you play with my hair, and that I can feel the paper cuts on your fingers when you trace the lines on my hands. I like that you prefer being permanently stuck in a storybook. I like that—"

Bash began to chuckle, and he put a hand up to stop me. "What's all this blandishment about?"

Sighing at the interruption, I rolled my eyes over his frilly language and leaned my head against his shoulder. "I just wanted to let you know. You say stuff like that to me all of the time."

He put an arm over me and pressed his lips to my temple. "Well, when you blush it's charming."

I grinned and squeezed out of the corner of the armchair to get a look at his face. Realizing what I was about to do, Bash snatched the book that was resting on his lap and held it in front of his face.

"No," he warned, his voice high. "No, Jovial."

I giggled and tried to move his hand from his face. "You're..." I tried to think of a pretentious word he would enjoy. "Nonsensical?"

He laughed at that and stopped fighting me by lowering the book so that I could see his clear blue eyes shining playfully. "You tried."

I scoffed and pushed him lightly. "Whatever. You sound just as ridiculous."

He lowered the book from his face and shook his head, forgetting his embarrassment now that there was an opportunity to turn the conversation elsewhere.

"Jovie, my love, it's an art." His voice purposely turned pompous the way he knew annoyed me, and I groaned the way he knew I would. "You're lovely even when you want to beat me with a book." He grinned.

I wrinkled my nose and he wrinkled it back before stealing a kiss.

"You would be in so much trouble if you were working today."

He shrugged, and pulled me closer by the waist. "Oh, I doubt it. My co-workers find us devastatingly sweet. Judy asked when I was going to propose." I felt the color drain from my face and my eyes widen, which only made Bash laugh and press a kiss to my cheek. "I had a similar reaction. Still, no amount of refutation could convince them otherwise."

My mouth went dry, and any attempt to say anything felt like it would come out in a stammering mess.

After a short hum, I forced a sentence out. "It's not like you've actually thought about something like that, right?"

It took a moment too long for him to reply, "When I think of the future, I think of something more immediate."

"What does that mean?"

My eyes were on our entwined feet, and I felt my body shift away from him as much as it could, considering we were crammed together.

"I—uh." He stumbled over the beginning of a few sentences, like he was fighting his tongue from spelling out what was on his mind. "Sometimes I imagine that you let me come with you to Manhattan. I like to ponder what that would be like — to stay with you."

I felt my entire body turn hot, like I was a wax candle melting from the intensity of the flame. "Oh."

"I would do it, you know? No questions asked. If you ever thought that was why we can't be together—"

"I told you why we can't," I reminded him robotically, realizing that this was turning into something I dreaded. "That has nothing to do with it. Don't make it harder than it is."

"Well," his voice suddenly snapped. "I apologize, Jovie, but I'm not like you. It's harder for me. It's comforting to know that this isn't going to end abruptly while I'm in the middle of loving you, but...I wish I could be there."

I wanted to tell him what Quinn had said. I wanted to reassure him that if it was meant to be, then we would find a way back to each other eventually. But, I knew who Bash was. He was hopelessly romantic in the kind of way that handicapped him. If he had hope, he would never move on. I couldn't hurt him like that. I didn't want him to wait for something that wasn't certain.

It pained me. I had grown to want too much, and the spinning wheel that I was came too close to completely toppling over for far too long. It was time I stopped daydreaming.

These were my first steps out of the clouds.

"I'm in the middle of loving you, too," I told him gently, raking a hand through his golden hair. "That's why I can't stay."

He grabbed my wrist, stopping me. "You are a paradox of a person, Jovial. Don't leave me, yet."

I searched his face, finding that all of the odd angles of his face seemed filed down and rounded like I had worn him out. Nobody ever tells you that love can do that. That one person can thrive while the other one begins to wilt. And, as that realization dawned on me, I felt sure I was making the right decision.

"Just kiss me for right now?" I asked, sliding my arm around his neck and pulling him close.

He didn't need an explanation, he just kissed me. He was day and I was night, and we could only be together as long as twilight would allow.

Now, only a sliver of a second remained.

Chapter 23

As graduation drew closer for some of us, final exams and research papers drew closer for the underclassmen. While some of us were celebrating, the underclassmen were introducing themselves to the city library for the first time that year. And, while that wouldn't necessarily be a problem for most people, it turned into the very thing that began putting space between Bash and I. Suddenly, he had people to assist with finding material suitable for a bibliography, and I started only seeing him after closing hours, or not at all.

In the beginning our lives slowly faded together, and now, just as slowly, they were being pulled apart. And, I guess that's the pattern of it all-if we allow it to happen, that is. Because, I had been allowing it to happen.

Truthfully, I was taking advantage of it all.

I think Bash saw it, too. He recognized the signs, started to smile in a way that told me he knew, kissed me extra long before I would leave, and tried to sway my decision with every gaze into my eyes and every breathy laugh into my ear.

When my graduation cap and gown arrived in the school office for me to pick up, I started to organize all of the gray things in my life back to black and white-for the sake of my sanity-for the sake of trying to be able to cope. Because, we all go back to the things that are familiar to us when we falter, after all.

There was something about holding that gown up to my shoulders in the mirror when I got home-something that made my breath catch. And, just like that, I knew it was time. I had to stop pretending, now.

But, I dreaded it. Every time Bash would run his fingers through my hair or say a silly word that was too embellished for the conversation or kiss me under the lamppost outside my house...I dreaded what had to come. I knew I wouldn't be able to do what was best for both of us without breaking something. Because, unlike bones, hearts don't heal so quick. It throbs for what feels like ages, and the regret makes the whole world seem blurry for a while.

And, yet, to save the hopeless romantic and push the closet romantic to fall in love with herself, for once, the whole messy ordeal had to be done.

"Today?" Quinn had asked as we biked down our street after school, feet idle on the pedals as we slowed before her house. She winced as the chickens began to squawk at us, even at this distance.

Her lovely hair was all thrown up in a knot, and her lipgloss shimmered in the light, but she frowned at me in a way that made the pretty disappear.

"Every time I look at the gown, I feel like I can't breathe. It's taunting me."

She snorted and shook her head. "Melodramatic, much? Just put it back in the box. Take advantage of your time with Bash. He's a diamond in the rough, if you ask me."

We stopped in her driveway and she crossed her arms when she looked at me. I looked down at my chipping toenail polish.

"The sooner this is over with, the sooner I can stop feeling bad about it-because I constantly feel awful," I told her, grimacing.

"Maybe that's your gut telling you it's the wrong move," she suggested as she swung her leg over and stood beside her bike. "Think about it."

"I have," I groaned. "Nobody gets it. This isn't a selfish move, it's for both of us. I care about him, that's why I'm doing this. He doesn't know he's hurting himself. He's blinded that way. He's like Henry."

"Great, then he'll never get over you." She smiled in a forced way that wasn't convincing.

My stomach flipped. "Don't say that."

She shrugged and began walking her bike up the drive. "I'll be here," she called over her shoulder. "If you need a good cry afterward."

I let out a shaky breath and pushed a hand through my frizzy, dark hair, feeling my fingers get caught in the tangles

Bash's fingers always seemed to avoid. The scowl appeared before I could stop it. My insides tightened, and a queasy, seasick feeling washed over me at the thought of what I was turning my bike around to go do.

Several large breaths later, I was wiping a tear off my flushed cheek and scolding myself for getting so upset. Life, I thought, liked to dangle things in front of me-liked to let my fingers brush against those wonderful things for just a moment before yanking it out of reach.

I thought the space I had been putting between Bash and I would make these next moments easier.

Oh, what a fool I had been.

The key was in the hanging plant and nobody was home. Bash would be at the library for an hour or so, yet, and I knew Greg was visiting family presently-which he made sure everyone knew in case he didn't return.

"I'm the least successful cousin," he said around a breath of smoke. "I'm certain I'll be torn to shreds. And, if that is the case, remember me with love in your hearts and please, smoke a cigarette in my memory."

I shook my head at the thought as I leaned backwards to close the door with my back. It is the last memory I would have of him-the last time his bad mood would seep into all corners of the room like the smoke he puffed on.

Since he insisted we smoke in his memory, and I would surely never see him again, I helped myself to the package he left on the book shelf.

The window opened with ease, and the element-faded slab of wood lifted off the Cigarette Graveyard with one hand. I lit the cigarette and sat down in the window, releasing smoke in a slow breath before looking back into Bash and Greg's apartment. I would never be a guest in it, again. And, that was a sad thought.

Sticky notes and loose books and half-drunk bottles of beer...I tried to record every last inch of it as perfectly as I could to memory. It was the physical haven I had come to when I needed it. But, it was time to let go of my life preserver.

Long after the cigarette, I stayed sitting in the window looking out at the mismatched houses of Bash's neighborhood: crumbling brick, boarded up windows, cheap lawn decorations. Not the clean, manicured grass of my neighborhood. Not the jolly singing of show tunes, or the squabble of chickens, or the bikini clad teenage girls swaying down the street to the waterpark.

It was quieter here, rougher, but somehow friendlier. Anyone was welcome.

Finally, I went to Bash's room where his mattress would forever remain on the floor and books would be everywhere but on his desk and sticky note reminders would clutter the back of his bedroom door. I returned the journals he let me borrow. I ran my fingers over the ones I hadn't gotten to read.

Out of curiosity, I pulled the latest one off the stack and flipped it to its most recent entry.

May 26th, 2015

There are but a few grains of sand left in this hourglass. How can I convince her to stay? How do I buy myself more time? She doesn't realize the power she has, doesn't understand what she's capable of. There is so much left of her I haven't gotten to experience. She says I have seen her soul, but there is more. She is forever an enigma. I am forever intrigued. I would forever remain hers if she let me.

But, she is elusive. She doesn't quite know herself, yet.

Is it fair of me? Am I suffocating the parts of her that need wide open fields of fresh air?

She is young, yet. I knew this. I wanted to show her the possibilities. But, can someone like me remain constant in a life as green as hers?

She thinks not. She is wiser than she appears.

I am all romantic notions and visions of life ideally.

Grow together or apart? I'm afraid the answer will break my heart. But, I asked for that didn't I?

I want to feel everything...right?

Signed,

Bash Daley

I swallowed hard and slammed the notebook shut, closing my eyes as my temples throbbed. And, just as I backed out of the room, Bash was walking through the front door. I jumped like I'd been committing a heinous crime in his absence, sure he would be able to see the guilt in my eyes.

He stopped on the welcome mat and slipped out of his shoes, staring at me with a cocked eyebrow.

"Jovie?"

I cleared my throat, but my voice still squeaked when I spoke. "Bash, hi."

I tried to smile, but the heaviness that settled into the muscles of my body settled into my smile, too.

He took a few steps forward and pressed a kiss to my lips, one that meant hello but felt like goodbye.

"What're you doing here?"

He walked past me into the living room where he set a stack of book onto the coffee table. I noticed he was avoiding eye contact, or staying near me in general.

Choking. It felt like I was choking, like the air was being squeezed from my lungs the longer my eyes stayed focused on him.

"I love you."

He glanced up. His body stilled, half bent over the coffee table, and his eyes settled on mine, but they were heavy. I think he had borrowed some of Quinn's intuition that day.

"What?"

He stood up straight, but every inch of him moved as though he was weighted down by tar, or stuck in a pool of cold molasses. It felt like being put in slow motion. He knew. The signs were there, the words I could never say were being said, and the smell of cigarettes hung in the air like something final.

"I love you," I said again, this time looking into the wide blue eyes that always felt like home.

I swear I saw color drain from his face. Those words weren't supposed to make a person feel sick.

"Jovie-"

"I'm leaving for New York shortly after graduation." I said quickly, cutting him off, trying to get the whole speech I prepared out as fast as I could. I couldn't stand there like that, lightheaded and on the brink of tears-feeling as though I was killing the very person I needed to stay alive.

"I know that," he said carefully, his voice void of the excitement that usually coated every word in a shiny varnish.

We stared at each other for a long moment until finally I told him, "I don't want to just end this and leave in a messy rush."

Bash let out a strangled half-chuckle, half-sigh and leaned back, pressing his palms against his closed eyes, trying to wake himself up from a nightmare. "Jovie," he said, sounding desperate. "I told you we don't have to end this. I will come with you."

"I don't want you to, Bash. I refuse to just uproot your life. You hate living in big cities, and I can't have you being miserable for me."

"I don't care about the city. I care about you."

"No, Bash," I nearly yelled, taking a few steps forward as he rounded the couch to do the same. "I need to be alone. I want a clean slate. That's why I'm leaving-that's why I've always wanted to leave-why I needed to leave. Bash, you belong here. I release you."

He threw his hands up. "Release me?" He shook his head and firmly gripped my shoulders. "I'm not a prisoner! What don't you understand? Why can't you bear the idea of somebody caring enough about you that they would do anything for you?"

"That's what I worry about," I nearly cried, pushing his hands off of me. "Please. You knew this was coming. Don't make this harder for me."

"It's hard because you know it isn't the answer." I swiped a stray tear away and began walking away from him, but he grabbed my arm and spun me around. His eyes were glassy, and his voice lacking luster. "Jovie, I believe this was meant to be."

I shook my head, sniffling. "Then why am I leaving, Bash?"

As I tried to tell him our time had run out, his hands were all over me, gripping my shoulders, cupping my face, pulling me closer, trying to find a way to keep me forever.

I pulled out of his grip again and took a step backward. "I just came to tell you that I love you, and that I need you to stop hanging on."

"Don't. Jovie. Don't. Please don't go." He begged.

I shook my head and took another step back, but he had reached a point of panic. And, in one final attempt to keep me, one final clinging effort, he swooped down and pressed a frantic kiss to my lips, all messy and tear-soaked and angry. He gripped onto me like I was fading into nothingness right before him.

As he pulled away, his hands pushed my hair back, and he searched my eyes, looking for something he would never find.

"I love you," I whispered. "That's why I have to go."

He released me suddenly, and the anger had finally taken over where understanding had always been. "You think that makes it better because it doesn't, Jovie. You're just twisting the blade," he fumed.

"Bash-"

He turned away from me, recoiling and yelling-hurt for all of the right reasons. Even I couldn't argue when the slow chocolate-melting voice boiled and hissed, "Leave then. Leave, Jovie!"

And I stumbled out of the house coughing, crying, melting, and jelly-legged.

He felt everything. I felt everything, too.

It felt like being set on fire, like being drowned, like falling off a cliff, like walking out of a daydream. It felt like rage, and sorrow, and a drug-induced sleepiness that makes you feel like night will last forever.

It felt like heartbreak. And, heartbreak was miserable.

And, that night while I lie in bed sobbing, I found Meredith tiptoeing in and lying down beside me to hold me as I cried.

"You're going to be okay," she murmured into my tear-soaked hair.

"I love him," I wailed, curling against her.

"I know," she sighed, hugging me tighter. "I know."

Chapter 24

Waking up from a daydream and walking into reality was something I felt in all the angles of my body and within the deepest parts of my mind. One moment I was riding the highest waves of tangible bliss, the next I was lying curled up in my bed with Luis purring on my chest and my limbs asleep and unwilling.

There was an emptiness, a space I had cut out specifically for Bash, that I had no experience fixing. I wanted him back, I craved the security of having him close, but everything I knew about love and life told me that it was over, that I had ended it, and that I needed to move forward. I had big plans for myself, and my summer distraction turned first real love was not an excuse to lose focus.

I had to repeat these things to myself over and over again to numb the sadness that lingered at the edge of all of my thoughts.

He is not an excuse.

Perhaps I was too young to understand the idea of sacrifice in a love like ours. Perhaps I was too wrapped up in the plans I had made for myself before Bash. I had my life figured out in bullet points and to-do lists. That's how I had grown up. And, when you're about to become independent—when you're about to do life all by yourself, people like me don't take risks.

People like me hold their heads high, smile through the pain, and cast what has been done over our shoulders to try and forget. We build armor and we go off to war.

I packed the things Bash gave me into a box: the hair elastic off his wrist, a stack of books the library was going to get rid of, a Leonard Cohen cassette he insisted I needed in my life, bits of half-written poetry he'd write while I studied, developed photos, and the sticky note that started it all among other things. I packed those things up and pushed it to the back of my closet. Just having them out of sight helped me pull myself back together—something Quinn was watching me struggle with.

"You know," she said the day before graduation as she painted my fingernails a deep blue to match our gowns. "He would take you back in a heartbeat."

"He told me to leave," I replied in a monotone voice while waving a freshly polished set of nails. "And rightfully so. I was so stupid going to his house and thinking we could have a conversation that would end in closure. But, no. Most of it was yelling and crying. Sloppy and unfinished. And I just feel awful about it all the time." I frowned deeply and took the nail polish from her. "I keep myself up at night cringing over the whole thing. I don't think I can ever look him in the eye, again."

Quinn's eyes were soft and sympathetic as she watched me ramble.

"He did something to you," she commented thoughtfully. "Something good. You're different now."

My brow furrowed. "I know. It makes everything harder."

She watched as I painted her nails for a moment and then took a breath. "Don't close back up, again—like before. Don't push people away like you used to."

I kind of smiled at that and looked her in the eye. "After what I did to Meredith? I have to lead by example, Quinn." I laughed softly. "I'm just prioritizing. Let me get settled in my new life outside of Ashwood Creek and I'll start experimenting, again. Who knows." I shrugged.

Quinn snorted. "So full of plans and expectations. You can't let your life fall apart when something doesn't happen the way you're anticipating."

"I know."

"Do you?"

I sighed heavily as I closed the nail polish bottle, using it as an excuse not to look at her.

"There's always Bash," I finally said. "I didn't plan on him and he ended up being everything I didn't know I wanted. So, if something in my life isn't going according to plan, I'll just think of Bash. Accidents, unexpected opportunities, detours...all of those things can be magic, too."

Quinn considered me for a moment, trying to find something genuine and honest in what I had said. And then, wet nails and all, she stretched across the table to hug me. She rarely smiled at me the way she was smiling now. It had never been a big deal before, but there was something satisfying about making her proud. She had always been like a sister to me, but that day was when I realized just how important she was. And, for the first time in days, I felt my heart warm.

"Who are you and what have you done to my Jo-Jo?"

Blushing, I shook my head and closed the gap between Henry and I in a short, tight hug, careful not to poke his eye out with my graduation cap. Meredith beamed at us, but straightened me out again after I let go of my father.

"You look lovely as well, Mer," Henry told her.

I glanced at her in her pearls and well-tailored dress with her hair curled smooth and her face etched in a perfect, seemingly permanent grin. Her cheeks warmed, much to my surprise, and I had to keep myself from gaping at her.

"I told you, it's Meredith or Miss Sinclair," she said a little stiffly after clearing her throat, eyes not meeting his.

Henry shook his head. "Oh, no, not today. Our daughter is graduating. Toss the formalities out the window, Mer, because this is a special occasion."

Meredith made several attempts at beginning a sentence and then gave up and smoothed down her skirt instead. "Fine."

I smiled at Henry, and he winked back.

There was something different about them since the whole blowup between Meredith and I. They were finally warming up to each other, or at least, Henry was trying again. And, Meredith, well, she wasn't protesting quite as hard. It was nice, sort of. All the tension that seemed to exist between them was fading, and I felt less uncomfortable standing between them. It felt like people weren't staring at us so much anymore. Being escorted into school like that was more than I could ever hope for. We felt like family.

The graduation ceremony was short and formal. Ashwood Creek isn't a big place, and they really know to organize efficient events that are frill-free. If it's going to cost people time, it's banned. If it's going to take away from the professionalism and formality of the ceremony, it's banned.

Some graduations have students cartwheeling towards their diploma or holding flash mobs.

Our school, inspired by my mother-mayor herself, rejected all of this.

In-and-out.

Name. Accomplishments. Diploma. The end.

So, when they announced us as official high school graduates, and our tassles were switched from right to left while the school song blared in the background, it felt quite sudden and a little bit surreal. Caps were tossed, the entire room exploded in applause, and suddenly I was lost in a sea of my peers with Quinn bouncing up and down across the gym towards me and a small weight lifted from my shoulders.

"We're done with high school, bitches!" Quinn cheered as she tackled me in an off-balanced hug while Zoey and Noel gathered around us, closing us in for a group hug.

I couldn't help it, I started laughing and bouncing along with them. Of the many steps in life that are deemed essential to success, I had ticked off one of the first, and I was absolutely flushed with excitement. And then, Quinn brought her lips to my ear and said the unthinkable.

"Bash is here."

My stomach dropped, and suddenly, I felt myself unable to move, unable to think.

Bash here? At my graduation? Attending the very ceremony that was the deadline for our relationship?

How?

I couldn't even think of facing him, much less catching a glimpse of him in the crowd. I felt embarrassed, foolish, immature, and completely heartbroken. He couldn't be here. If I felt awful, I couldn't imagine what he was going through.

Still, as the girls all let go of me, I looked up into the bleachers and scanned the families standing up and coming down to find their graduates. But, he wasn't there. It wasn't until I looked toward the corner, at the end of the bleachers near the door, that I found Bash standing in his work clothes, hair fastened in a tight bun, and hands in his pockets staring at me.

I held my breath when he met my eye, but the corners of his lips rose softly and he nodded at me.

"Go."

I looked back at Quinn and the girls who were all watching me with palpable interest.

I didn't say anything, just let my heart guide my feet to where Bash stood.

He watched calmly until I was standing in front of him, and then he motioned for me to follow him outside. Everything in my head was fuzzy, and I followed without question.

The cool breeze was a refreshing change of atmosphere since I'd been sweating in the muggy, overcrowded gymnasium for a little over two hours. And, that cool breeze was all I needed to wake up.

"Bash, I'm sorry," I said as quickly as the door shut behind us and before the smell of freshly mown grass could reach my nose. "I'm sorry that it ended that way."

Sighing, Bash held up a hand to stop me from going any further. His eyes were tired, not wide and sparkling like I had always known them to be.

"I just came to say congratulations and I hope that your life is everything you want it to be."

It's horrible the way people say some things some times. This was particularly awful because I could hear in his voice just how hard it was to say that to me. I would have done nearly anything in that moment to get his voice to be slow-melting chocolate again and for his eyes to shimmer mischievously and for his infamously aloof body language to return.

"You are the greatest person I've ever known," I told him, my voice shaking. "And I'm sorry I'm the way that I am. And, if I had met you in a different life there is no doubt in my mind that I would do anything to make forever a reality."

He smiled in a watery way that a person does when they want to cry. "No, don't be sorry. You have to do this, Jovie. I would hate for you to resent me in the future because I didn't allow you to grow independently as a person. People need that, I needed that. I get it. But, if I had met you in a different life I would have asked you to marry me, and it's thrilling to know that there is a possibility you would have said yes."

Relief is a wonderful thing, and I felt that when he told me that he understood—that I was, in a sense, forgiven. He made me want to experience our entire love story all over again.

I took his hands in mine and gazed up into his eyes with as much sincerity as I could muster. "Thank you for the adventure, Sebastian Daley the Third."

His face turned blotchy and he turned it away bashfully, as always, trying to convince me he wasn't blushing. But, after taking a deep breath, he was able to look at me, again.

"It has been a pleasure learning all of the things that make you unequivocally mesmeric. Thank you for giving me the opportunity."

And that's when I kissed him one final time. I felt the last of his papercut fingers sliding across my skin, and smelled the last of his amber cologne on his clothes, freedom and desire encircled us in one final embrace, and a craving I had gotten so familiar to satisfying received its final allowance. His lips on mine, they tasted like the last few moments of first love.

No other person in my life has ever recreated the things I experienced with my first love. No other person has loved me the way that Bash did, has given me the confidence to be whatever I wanted to be.

They say to stop talking about how my life changed after him.

I think there are many factors that contributed to my awakening, and he just happened to be my favorite part. Love, some say, can change the world. Whether it is romantic or otherwise, it spurs something in us, something special. It's the purest form of human compassion and understanding and commitment.

When our worlds are not in chaos, what could be better to stir up our simple lives than a whirlwind of love? It is more powerful than anything else, so much so that the phrase "swept off my feet" is too gentle.

He was not everything, but he was something. If anything, he was an indulgence that I still savor.

Epilogue

Present Day

The streets of New York City are swarming with people. Always. It's one of the many things that drew me to the area after living in Ashwood Creek. The constant buzz of police sirens and the instant gift of invisibility in a place as intimidating as the city had me packing my bags.

Past the flash and the glamor and the concrete jungle mayhem, there is something perfectly simple about life here. The stress of having to be perfect seems to vanish in a world as chaotic as this. And, while most people heave in anxiety, I sink back and relax into a world so unlike the small town I grew up in. I get the bigger picture, somehow.

I walk everywhere here the same way I biked everywhere in Ashwood Creek. I've never lived in a place that required any other sorts of transportation, and it's the kind of thing that keeps me thinking about home.

Home, where Meredith and Henry are. There's a note on my fridge reminding me to call Meredith and another telling me that Quinn's baby is due this month. If someone would have told me six years ago that these are the kind of things that would be important to me, I wouldn't have believed you for a second.

But, the reality of this life is that if you don't hold onto the people who love you, it's going to be a lonely journey. After breaking up with Bash all those years ago, I felt that loneliness. And, to help me cope, I filled the pages of that journal I requested as a birthday gift from Quinn. I filled those pages with the story of Bash and I. The ups, the downs, an explanation for the decisions I made and why, the fondest memories, my favorite words. And then, because I had snooped into his journals and read all of the personal entries he would let me, I sent my journal to Bash to return the favor.

He replied with a short letter that read:

Jovie,

You cannot possibly understand how grateful I am for your journal. You have given me a key with which to unlock the world. Thank you.

-Bash

I still don't understand just what he meant by his letter, but I was glad he got it. It was therapeutic to me, writing that journal, and by doing it I realized just how Bash remained as composed and cheerful as he did.

The mind is a cluttered place, and straightening everything out through writing offers serenity.

Despite the many detours and accidents it took to get where I am, I'm happy. Even as the sun bakes the pavement and the humid waves of heat cook me as I walk past a row of darkly painted buildings, I'm not disappointed with the way things turned out for me.

Well, at least, that's what I tell myself as I push past an oddly dense crowd of people on Crosby Street. When your bobby pins are falling out of place and you're trying not to sweat through your white blouse, being swarmed by this many people as though it's Times Square is the last thing you want to deal with. And, trust me, I've dealt with a a lot of bullshit today.

"Hey, Miss, what do you think you're doing?"

I blow a frizzy strand of hair from my face and turn toward the older gentleman with as much patience as I can gather.

"Excuse me?"

"You're breaking up the whole line."

I blink in confusion. "What line?"

"Didn't you see the sign back there?" the man asks hoarsely. "This side of the street is closed. The Bookstore Café is holding a signing."

I look back down the crowded street with furrowed brows and then glance up at the bookstore. Who the hell attracts a crowd like this? I just want to get home and call Meredith and check in on Quinn. Is that too much to ask for?

"A signing?" I ask, not quite believing him. "Is JK Rowling here?"

"No." A woman whom I assume is the man's wife by the color coordinated attire holds up a book for me to see. "Sebastian Daley."

The name causes my scowl to melt into a look of stunned paralysis. "S-Sebastian who?" I stammer.

The woman gives me a funny look, but hands me the book she's holding so that I can look at it. And, there it is, all in gold, cursive calligraphy: Sebastian Daley. But, that has to be a coincidence, so I flip the back cover open to get a look at the author. And, sure enough, there is a resemblance in this man and the man I knew six years ago. If I stare long enough at the photo, I can see his eyes sparkle and the blush bloom across his cheeks.

I turn the book back to the cover.

At the Corner of I Love You and Goodbye

I can't take my eyes off the cover, it feels like they'll be stuck there forever. "What's the name of the love interest?"

"Uhm..." The woman hesitates. She must think I'm crazy. "Joslyn."

Joslyn, I think. Of course it's Joslyn. I feel a little lightheaded standing here, but also like I've been shocked. I don't care about getting home anymore, I don't care that the heat has turned my hair into a bird's nest or that my day was less than wonderful. All I can think is that Bash is here-and not just here, but that the only thing between myself and seeing him again are all of these people.

The last I heard from him was that letter, but I still think about him every day. I fall out of relationships, I put all of my energy into my work, I read an old novel when I get homesick for the first person that made me feel anything real at all. And...here he is.

It makes me think of something Quinn said a long time ago.

And, like tunnel vision, the only thing on my mind is seeing him.

"Thank you," I mutter to the couple as I hand back the book. But, that's where my manners find their end.

I push through the line, ignoring the cussing and protesting of those waiting in it. And, when I reach the stairs, my heart nearly gives out when I notice the sign in the window.

Book Signing with New York Times #1 Best-Selling Novelist Sebastian Daley

Then, it's all elbows and ducking around limbs-something you become a professional at when you've lived in a big city long enough-until I'm standing in a crowded room of buzzing conversation and massive shelves of books.

That's when I see him again for the first time.

He sits behind a low table, lips turned up in a grin as he listens to the request of a reader before signing across the title page of his book. I barely recognize the young man I fell in love with all of those years ago. He's a real grown-up now with a squarer jaw that complements all of the angles of his face. His hair is cropped short and he has more than just a bit of morning stubble. The button-down shirts are no longer dress-code. He suits twenty-six more than twenty.

And, maybe it's a horrible cliché, but as I continue to make my way towards him, the whole world seems to slow around me-like the rest of the world has faded into the background and there's nothing and no one but him and me.

Then, he glances up, and for a moment he sees me and then he turns to the next waiting person in the line. But, then he pauses and finds me again, standing just a few feet away all flustered and a little unsightly from the humidity.

The genuine surprise on his face causes a shy smile to form on mine.

"Hi," I say.

He just stares.

We look at each other for another hard moment, contemplating one another, looking for some kind of message in the other person's eyes that says "I've moved on" or "I'm not the same person I used to be."

No such message comes or goes, but I still find myself holding my breath.

Bash looks to the young girl who is waiting for his signature, and she looks over her shoulder at me curiously, wondering who I am and why I'm holding up the line.

"Can you excuse me for a moment?" he asks her. She shrugs.

Bash meets my eyes, again. My legs might give out I'm so nervous.

"Do you believe in fate, yet?"

It wasn't until the sun started to go down that the line dwindled into nothing and Bash was finally able to leave the book store. He insisted I stay and wait for him to finish, and there was no arguments on my end. While I waited I started to read his book. It was honest, and heartbreaking, and raw right from the start. But, the most intriguing thing for me was seeing our relationship from his perspective. Not even in the name of fiction did he ever anger with me-he always tried to understand things from my perspective, but you could read the heartbreak between the lines. That was, perhaps, the most addictive thing about the book.

"I can't believe you wrote a book." My voice seems to be stuck in the permanent tone of awe.

We walk side-by-side over the bumps and cracks of the broken sidewalk, unsure of where we are headed or even if we have a destination. It seems as though we're content to wander as long as we can be together.

I haven't felt this way since Ashwood Creek. Every single teenage flurry of admiration I once held for him seems to swirl, and tumble, and dance within me all at once. And, it's not overwhelming, it's comfortable. It's new and familiar all at once. Everything from his voice to the smell on his clothes brings me back to a time when forever was a fantasy.

He shrugs off what I said in the modest way that he did six years ago whenever I tried to compliment him. Even to this day he can't understand his own brilliance, or is too flustered to acknowledge it.

"I remembered what my grandad said about not wanting to be forgotten," he tells me. "And looking back through our journals made me realize that I couldn't bear that, either. So, I decided to put it in print."

"You made our love immortal," I say into the sticky air between us, eyes on the pinks and oranges of the sky un-blocked by tall buildings.

"I'm sorry. I didn't mean for it to be creepy," he says quickly, blushing and stuttering in a way that makes my lips turn up. "It's just that writers are at their best when they work with something meaningful. It's art. I needed the closure."

I know his cheeks are red, but I don't look at him. I keep my eyes to the sky and continue to ask him questions, eager to hear him talk more-to focus on the first thing I fell in love with. "So, why Sebastian Daley? Why not Bash?"

He takes the opportunity to recover and clears his throat. "In honor of the first Sebastian, my grandad. He's the one who inspired me first. I thought we could share a name on the cover."

"That's beautiful," I say, softly.

He shook his head. "Alright, I'll let that one go."

"What?"

"Beautiful."

"Oh, no. Really?" I laugh. "You still don't like that word? What would you prefer I said?

"You know I don't like that word," he banters back. "It's so unoriginal. How about...charming, stunning, enchanting....a nything else."

"That's just ridiculous," I tell him and roll my eyes. But, I'm smiling widely, and we're walking so close our arms brush despite the wide sidewalk.

We look at each other like we're standing in the library that first day and we're both unsure yet oddly intrigued. Six years is a long time, and we don't quite know what's going to happen next.